ALL MY TOMORROWS

Jessica was in the middle of a revolution, but as a doctor she couldn't refuse to shelter the wounded American journalist who turned up at her door, even at the risk of her own life. But it wasn't the physical danger that frightened her—she was afraid of falling in love ...

Books you will enjoy
by ROSEMARY HAMMOND

MALIBU MUSIC

Gerry had promised Bianca that their friendship would be platonic. But for how long could a man like Gerry keep such a promise? And what was it that he was hiding from her?

LOSER TAKES ALL

Cara was the bride Nicholas Curzon had won in a poker game ... winner take all ... But he couldn't take away her revulsion at his love-making, or her pride. Her life was as empty of purpose as their marriage was of love—she had to keep her heart and self-respect or she would lose everything.

PLAIN JANE

When chance threw Jane into the arms of the handsome Blake Bannister, her normally ordered world was turned upside down as she struggled to make sense of the feelings threatening to take control of her life.

ALL MY TOMORROWS

BY

ROSEMARY HAMMOND

MILLS & BOON LIMITED
15–16 BROOK'S MEWS
LONDON W1A 1DR

*First published in Great Britain 1986
by Mills & Boon Limited*

© Rosemary Hammond 1986

*Australian copyright 1986
Philippine copyright 1987
This edition 1987*

ISBN 0 263 75550 9

*Set in Times 10½ on 11 pt.
01-0187-48159*

*Computer typeset by SB Datagraphics,
Colchester, Essex*

*Printed and bound in Great Britain by
Collins, Glasgow*

CHAPTER ONE

THE sound of the guns had begun to get on Jessica's nerves. Inside the surgery, it was only a low distant rumble, like the thunder from the surrounding mountains she had become so accustomed to in her year in San Cristobal, but now the gunfire seemed to be coming closer every day, and she was beginning to wonder if Marshall Bennett hadn't been right. Maybe she should think seriously about going home.

Yet she hated to give up so soon, she thought, as she gazed out into the village square that evening before locking up. She had come to the tiny Central American republic with such high hopes and a firm intention to help the villagers. Fresh out of her internship in family practice and filled with a crusader's zeal, she had wanted more than anything to use her medical skill for the poor people of this revolution-torn country.

She opened the heavy wooden front door and went outside on to the low cement stoep. The booming sounds immediately got louder. All the residents were inside their huts, the doors shut tight. It used to be that at sunset the square would be full of people, women gossiping at the market stalls, the men drinking outside the small *taverna* on the far side, the beautiful little brown children playing games in the dust. Now, and for the past week, it was empty.

Jessica sighed and went back inside. The sun would be gone in a few minutes, and the darkness would descend. It had taken her months to get used to that utter pitch darkness. Here in the valley of the mountains, there were no street lights, no neon signs, no brightly lit houses or shops. The only electricity here came from the generator at the nearby coffee plantation where most of the men of the village worked.

She bolted the door firmly behind her and went into the ground-floor surgery to clean up after a long, hard day's work. Even now, she thought, with the fighting still several miles away, she had had to remove more than one bullet from a young soldier, brought to her by a tearful mother or the local priest.

Even Marshall had admitted that she was probably in no real danger, however. At least not yet, she added as she put the gleaming steel instruments into the steriliser. She was totally non-political. Ever since she had come to San Cristobal there had been a revolution going on and guerrilla warfare in the mountains, but it had never affected her or her work before; she didn't even know what they were fighting about or what each side wanted. It was more like a dangerous national sport than a life and death struggle.

Yet it *was* a matter of life and death, and that fact was daily becoming clearer to her. She had patched up enough wounds on the young soldiers—just boys, really—to know that it was no game. And this time, even though she was the only doctor within a hundred miles and necessary to both sides, it was coming a little too close for comfort.

She finished in the surgery and went into her small office across the hall to go through her charts, making notes to herself as she flipped through the folders. Mrs Morales' baby was due any day now, and she needed to make sure the woman understood the simple rules of hygiene she had been teaching a local group of pregnant women. The Silva boy's cast could come off tomorrow, and Manuel's stitches were ready to be taken out.

She worked for a good two hours, the only time that she was relatively free of the constant demand for her services. In each file she saw not only her neat medical annotations, but also, in her mind's eye, a picture of the person. That was the important thing to her in medicine—the person. It was the only thing. Young Mrs Morales with the trusting, liquid brown eyes; little Pablo Silva, dragging around the cast on his leg for the past six weeks; and poor old Manuel, whose knife had slipped and sliced open his hand.

These people trust me, she thought fiercely, as she placed the folders in a neat pile on her desk. They are why I came here in the first place, and I'm not going to leave them, not until I'm virtually driven out!

She switched off the lamp and went upstairs to her living quarters. It was pitch dark outside now, so she turned on lights as she went. She would fix herself a little supper, she decided, then go back down and finish up with the files. If she was lucky, there would be no emergency to interrupt her tonight.

The next morning, as Jessica unbolted her front door and gazed out into the sunlit square, the guns seemed even louder. She had heard them during the night, but had been so tired by the time she finally dropped into bed that the muffled sounds didn't disturb her sleep.

Now, however, they seemed to be quite close. It was difficult to judge distances here in the wide valley merely from sound. It tended to bounce off the sides of the steep mountains that surrounded the village, and besides, until the shooting had started, there were no night sounds. Only the familiar shrieks of the birds or chatter of monkeys high in the banana trees broke the stillness then, and she had become accustomed to them.

Glancing around the square, she noticed that the villagers were still making themselves scarce. She also noticed, with a little thrill of alarm, that at the far end, in front of the *taverna* and near the church, was a small encampment of soldiers in uniform. As she stared, a man left the group and came walking toward her.

He was short and swarthy, a typical San Crístobal native, with a full black moustache and wearing a filthy uniform of some kind. As he approached, she instinctively shrank back, and had to fight the impulse to run inside the sanctuary of her house and bolt the door.

'You are the *medico*—the doctor?' he asked in English.

'Yes,' said Jessica, 'I am.'

'I am Captain Varga. I have many wounded men.' He gestured with his hand towards the group of soldiers, which seemed to be growing larger as he spoke. 'Fighting men of the glorious revolution.' He eyed her narrowly, as though to gauge her reaction to his announcement.

'I know nothing about the revolution,' she said. She was frightened, but she knew it would be a mistake to let this man see it. 'I am a doctor—I heal the sick and tend the wounded, that's all.'

He opened his mouth as though to object, then nodded abruptly. 'You will tend my men,' he said in a clipped voice, and stalked off.

All that day, Jessica stitched and cleaned and

bandaged the wounded soldiers, until by evening, she was exhausted. She was also worried about her dwindling supplies. The penicillin was getting low, and she had used more bandages in one day than she had in the past six months. She was also concerned about her regular patients, who were staying ostentatiously away while the soldiers trickled in and out of the surgery door.

Captain Varga had intimated that as soon as all his men were patched up and well enough to travel, they would be on their way. Apparently the enemy, whoever that might be, was close behind, and Jessica resigned herself to a brand new influx of wounded from the other side. She only hoped there wouldn't be any fighting in the village itself.

For the next two days, she pushed herself to work long hours, starting at sunrise and not stopping until the sun went down behind the western rim of the mountain range, hoping to get them out of the village as soon as possible. The stream of men seemed endless. They were a stoic people, though, and she could work quickly.

On the third day, Marshall Bennett drove up in his jeep from the capital, two hours away on the unpaved mountain roads. Jessica was standing at the window of her office gulping down a quick lunch when she saw him, and she was so delighted that she gave a glad involuntary cry and ran to the front door to let him in.

As she threw the door open, however, the cry died on her lips when she saw the group of soldiers surrounding his jeep, with Captain Varga in command and every man pointing an ugly, wicked-looking rifle at the man in the driver's seat.

'My name is Marshall Bennett,' she heard him say.

'I am with the American embassy in the capital. I am a diplomat, not a spy.'

Captain Varga spat contemptuously on the ground at those words and, poking Marshall with his rifle, he nudged him out of the jeep, forcing him to stand with his hands in the air while another soldier searched him.

Jessica had had enough. She was just about ready to run down and give Captain Varga a piece of her mind, when she caught Marshall's eye. He very slightly shook his head, and she stopped short. He knew what she had been about to do and was warning her off. She just stood there then, watching, as Captain Varga glanced through the papers in Marshall's wallet.

Then, grudgingly, he handed the wallet back to Marshall. He issued a crisp order in Spanish, and the guns were lowered. All eyes followed the tall, fair American, then, as he moved slowly, cautiously towards Jessica, still standing in the doorway,

'Let's go inside,' he said to her under his breath. 'Very slowly.'

When she had shut the door behind him, he gripped her by the arms and gazed down at her with grave concern in his eyes. 'Jessica, you've got to get out of here,' he said firmly.

'I don't think they'll let me,' she replied. 'They need me.'

He thought a minute. 'You're probably right. As soon as they're gone, though, you've got to get out. It's time to leave the country. This thing is escalating far beyond the minor skirmish we all thought it would be.'

'What do you mean?' she asked, alarmed.

'A few Americans have been killed,' said Marshall

Benett grimly. 'A reporter and a priest. It's getting out of hand. The government is about to topple, and then there will be chaos. Both sides think all Americans are spies.'

'Are you going to leave?'

'No; the embassy will be safe enough. But I want you out. The ambassador has issued an order to evacuate all Americans.'

She nodded. 'I'm no heroine, Marshall. I'll leave as soon as I can.'

'Good. I think you'll probably be okay here for a while, at least so long as they need you. I'll come back up, or send someone, probably in a week or so—whenever I can. You be all packed and ready to go at a moment's notice.'

Mrs Morales had her baby that night, and as Jessica dragged herself home around midnight after a safe delivery, she felt a sense of real accomplishment.

It was why she had chosen family practice as a speciality in the first place, she thought as she sat at her desk filling in the chart on Mrs Morales and listening to the distant gunfire. To help bring life into the world and then to nurture it, to help it mature and grow properly, gave her a sense of fulfilment and satisfaction that no other more exotic branch of medicine could.

She was so pleased at the successful delivery of the healthy, squalling new little Morales that she even forgot her fears for a moment. But just then, an especially loud, and quite close, burst of machine-gun fire startled her out of her euphoria, so that she dropped her pen and half rose out of her chair, her heart pounding.

I am afraid, she thought, as she sank back down

and pushed the file away. And Marshall's right. I must leave. The prospect saddened her. She had come to love the people of San Crístobal, but she knew the time had come. Marshall was not an alarmist; he wouldn't insist that she leave unless he was certain she was in real danger, or would be soon.

She had done what she could, she thought, as she wearily cradled her head in her arms on top of the desk. She had taught them the rudiments of hygiene and nutrition at least, and that was something. She closed her eyes, enjoying the sudden lull in the sounds of warfare, and was just beginning to drift off into a doze when she heard a tapping sound at her window.

Suddenly alarmed and fully awake, she switched off the desk lamp and walked cautiously over to the window. It came again, a low scratching noise this time. She pulled the curtain aside. It was pitch dark, with no moon, and she could see absolutely nothing, but just below the window, in the low pomegranate bushes, she could make out the bulky shape of a crouching man.

She didn't know what to do. There wasn't a sign of life inside the square, but far on the other side, near the *taverna*, a lone sentry trudged slowly back and forth in front of the flickering fire that burned near the soldiers' encampment. Slowly, she unlatched the window and opened it a crack.

'Who is it?' she whispered.

'Let me in,' came the low voice of a man. 'I'm hurt.'

There was no trace of an accent in his speech. Then, she thought, Marshall! Could he have been ambushed on the way back to the capital and come back? She made up her mind. Whoever it was, he was obviously an American and hurt. She was a doctor. She had to help.

She opened the window wide and leaned her head down. 'Can you make it to the door?' she whispered. 'It's so dark they won't see you.'

For answer, the shape half rose and started to creep stealthily to the door. Jessica ran into the hall and unbolted it carefully, so as not to make any noise. Then she pulled it open, and he half fell across the threshold into her arms.

It wasn't Marshall, she saw immediately. This man was quite a bit taller and had very dark hair. He was clutching his right arm with his left hand, and in the dim hall light, she could see that the sleeve of his khaki shirt was torn and covered with blood. Quickly and quietly, she shut and bolted the door behind him. As she did so, she glanced across the square at the soldiers' camp. The solitary sentry was leaning up against the wall of the *taverna* smoking a cigarette, and there was no other sign of activity among the sleeping men.

Supporting the man with one arm around his waist and the other holding his good left arm, she started to lead him into the surgery, but then she stopped to reconsider. Captain Varga and his men would be in and out all day, sometimes even in the middle of the night. He obviously didn't want to be seen. There was an extra bedroom upstairs; she would have to get him up there somehow.

'Do you think you can make it up the stairs?' she asked in a low voice.

He was leaning heavily up against her, and his face appeared haggard and full of pain. He gave her a groggy, dazed look and swayed a little on his feet.

'I can try,' he said at last in a weak voice.

Slowly, they began to climb the stairs, one agonising step after another. He was growing weaker, she could tell, and seemed much heavier, with at least half his weight on her for support. He was breathing in short rasps by the time they reached the top landing, and she began to worry that he might have internal injuries.

If so, she thought grimly as she led him into the small back bedroom, there was nothing much she could do for him outside of a hospital. The closest one was in the capital, more than a hundred miles away, and no way to get there.

Before turning on the light, she eased him down on a chair by the door of the bedroom and went to the one small window to make sure the curtains were drawn shut. She pulled the heavy white spread off the bed and draped it securely over the metal rod, tucking it in at the bottom and sides to make sure not a chink of light would show on the outside.

She turned on the bedside lamp, then, and went back to her strange visitor. Now that he was off his feet, he looked a little better, and she began to hope that his injuries were not quite as serious as she had feared. He was sitting sprawled on the wooden chair, his head resting back against the stucco wall, his long legs braced on the floor, and still clutching his wounded arm. His eyes were closed, and although his face still looked gaunt, his colour was not quite so ashen under the heavy tan.

'Will you be all right for a minute?' she murmured, bending over him. 'I've got to get some things from my surgery.'

His eyes fluttered open, and he struggled to focus on her. 'You're the doctor?' he asked weakly.

'Yes. I'll only be a minute. We mustn't make a sound, though. The soldiers are everywhere.'

He nodded and closed his eyes again. 'I

understand.'

She ran downstairs to the surgery and picked up some clean linen, her instrument bag and a supply of penicillin. When she got back upstairs, she threw the clean sheet over the bed and laid her equipment down on the table. Then she went back to the man.

'Come on,' she said. 'I'll help you to the bed.'

Somehow, she got him pulled out of the chair and over to the bed. He was a very large man, she thought as they stumbled together across the room, and quite heavy for her to support.

She eased him down on the side of the bed, and he sat there, swaying slightly, as she knelt in front of him and started unbuttoning his torn shirt. He looks strong enough, she thought as she slipped the shirt off his broad shoulders, not heavily muscled, but sinewy and supple. His chest and shoulders were damp with perspiration, which could indicate either exhaustion or infection or both.

She took off his heavy, mud-encrusted boots, then lifted his legs up on to the bed and eased him back into a prone position. He was clutching his arm again, and although it didn't appear to be bleeding any more, there was still so much old blood and dirt that she knew she would have to clean him up thoroughly before she could accurately assess the extent of his wound.

She went into the bathroom across the hall and filled a metal basin full of hot soapy water and found a clean flannel. She sat down on the edge of the narrow bed, leaned over him and began bathing his upper body, gently but firmly disengaging his hand from the wounded arm so that she could take a better look at it.

'It looks like a bullet wound,' she said. 'If the bullet

is still in there, I'll have to take it out.'

He looked up at her. 'It's still in there,' he said grimly.

For the first time since he had come to her door, she took a good look at him, and the first thought that crossed her mind was that she must have been insane to let a strange man into her house. His eyes were wild and bloodshot, his dark hair matted and tangled, and several days' growth of black stubble covered his unshaven cheeks and chin. His clothes were filthy, and he looked very much like one of the outlaws who roamed the mountains preying on travellers.

'Who are you?' she whispered.

'I'm an American,' he mumbled weakly. 'They think I'm a spy.'

'Who thinks you're a spy?'

He made a feeble attempt at a grin. 'Both sides do. Take your pick.'

He closed his eyes then, with a grimace of pain, and a sheen of perspiration broke out on his forehead. She rinsed out the cloth and bathed his face. She remembered what Marshall had told her about the two Americans who had been shot. This man is hurt, she thought, and he needs my help. What should I do, turn him out into the street and let the soldiers capture him and shoot him? She put her fears behind her and set to work.

'I'll have to remove the bullet first,' she said when she had finished examining the wound. She reached for her bag. 'You'll need an anaesthetic.'

His eyes flew open. 'No!' he said. 'No anaesthetic.'

'It's only novocaine,' she said as she adjusted the needle. 'I can't work on you without it. You won't be unconscious, if that's what you're worried about.'

He still wasn't satisfied, but was too weak to protest further. She gave him the novocaine, then, while it was taking effect, she swabbed the wound and the surrounding area with alcohol and gently explored the rest of his body for signs of internal injury.

As her fingers travelled deftly and expertly over him, she couldn't help noticing how finely built he was. The muscles of his chest and arms were solid, but lithe and athletic, and hard without being bulky. When she undid the buckle of his belt and slid the stained trousers down a little lower over his lean hips so that she could examine him further, the abdomen was flat and hard as a board.

When she was satisfied that he had no further injuries, she cleaned the wound on his arm again and set to work to extract the bullet. It hadn't gone very deep, and in less than a minute, it was out. She took a few stitches and bandaged the arm, then held the bullet up so that he could see it.

But he was unconscious by now, worn out from the shock of his wound, the fever from an obvious infection and the loss of strength expended in getting to her house on foot. He had also lost a lot of blood. She gave him two shots, one of penicillin for the infection and another to make him sleep through the night. She didn't want him to wake up and start raving in a delirium if his fever grew worse.

She covered him with a light blanket and then gathered up her things and stood beside the bed looking down at him. His breathing sounded even and peaceful enough. He was a strong, healthy man, not a boy, but still young. She would guess at least thirty-five, although it was hard to tell with the ravages of pain and the beard on his face.

She turned out the light and went back down to the surgery, where she cleaned up so that there would be no trace of him anywhere when the soldiers came in the morning, even mopping up the blood on the tile floor of the entry hall and stairs.

When she was through, it was quite late, after two o'clock in the morning, and she was totally exhausted from the long eventful day. She had learned when she was in medical school to get along on very little sleep, but then, she thought wryly as she trudged wearily back up the stairs, medical school was never like this!

She looked in on him once more on her way to her bedroom. His arms were outside the covers, his head turned to one side on the pillow, and he was breathing deeply and evenly. His forehead was still damp and quite warm to the touch, but by morning the antibiotic should start to take effect.

She went into her room, undressed and crawled into bed. She fell asleep almost instantly, but in the few seconds before she did, her thoughts centred on the stranger in her house. Who is he, she wondered, and how did he get here?

The next morning, she awoke to a strange silence. She sat up in bed, still half asleep, trying to figure out what it meant. Then she realised that there was no gunfire. She jumped out of bed and ran to her window, hoping to see that the soldiers had left, but when she pulled the curtain aside and peered out across the square, she could see that they were still there.

She put on a robe and went in to check on her patient. He was still sound asleep. When she felt his pulse, it was strong and regular, and although his face and shoulders were bathed in perspiration, he felt definitely cooler to her. His colour was a little better, too, and in the light of day, sleeping so peacefully, he didn't seem nearly as menacing and dangerous to her as he had last night.

She went into the bathroom across the hall and showered, then got dressed in her own room. In the year that she had been in San Crístobal, she had been so busy with the never-ending demands on her time that she had paid no attention whatsoever to her appearance. Her clothes were virtually interchangeable and consisted of denim skirts, light cotton blouses and sandals. For convenience, she had given up make-up entirely and worn her long, honey-coloured hair, bleached almost golden by the sun, pulled severely back from her face and twisted into a simple loose knot at the back of her head.

This morning, however, she looked into her cracked bedroom mirror for the first time in days, possibly weeks. She, too, was tanned by the tropical sun of San Crístobal and had a good colour, but she looked much thinner than she remembered and the girlish look was gone.

Then she thought, why am I doing this? Her greenish-hazel eyes stared back at her in amazement, and she turned away abruptly from her reflection. She never bothered about her appearance around Marshall, and he was the closest thing to a romantic interest she had experienced since college days. She had to laugh at that. The mild flirtation had been entirely on his part, and her few excursions with him into the capital for dinner or a party at the embassy had generated in her nothing warmer than grateful friendship for him.

As she walked down the hall to check on her

patient one more time before starting her daily
rounds, she wondered if he had anything to do with
her sudden interest in what she looked like. But that
was ridiculous, she decided. She didn't even know
him or anything about him. He could even be a spy or
an outlaw for all she knew.

He was awake when she got there, but only just, his
head propped up against the pillows, the blanket
down around his waist. When she entered the
bedroom, his eyes fastened on her, and for the first
time she noticed the odd colour. They were a very
dark slate-blue, and they were the coldest, hardest
eyes she had ever seen.

Once more, she felt that small unmistakable chill
that told her this man was dangerous. He menaced
her in a way she couldn't understand, and for a
moment she hesitated in the doorway. Then she
recognised the signs of physical weakness in him—
the haggard cheeks, the lines of suffering around his
thin set mouth—and she softened toward him.
Thinking of him as her patient gave her the
confidence she needed, and she walked briskly over
to the bed.

'How do you feel?' she asked in her most
professional manner.

He glanced up at her. 'Better,' he said curtly.

She shook down a thermometer and put it in his
mouth, then took his wrist to check his pulse. He
closed his eyes and lay very still while she worked
over him.

'You are better,' she said when she was through.
'Your pulse is strong and your fever is down.'

'When can I leave?' he asked, opening his eyes
again and glancing up at her.

'Not for several days,' she said. 'You've lost a lot of

blood and are still weak. I had to put stitches in your arm, and they'll need to come out before you can be fully active again.'

'I can't stay here,' he said flatly. 'Not with Varga's men in and out all day. I'll leave tonight.'

'Where will you go?'

He shrugged his broad shoulders, then winced as the pain of his wound shot through him. He closed his eyes again. 'I don't know,' he muttered. 'Maybe try to make it to the capital.'

'You wouldn't last a mile in your condition,' she stated firmly.

He gave her a sardonic look. 'What would you suggest, then? Turn me over to Varga and let them shoot me as a spy?'

'Are you?' she asked hesitantly. 'A spy?'

He laughed humourlessly in a short dry bark. 'Hardly! I'm a reporter. I'm down here in this god-forsaken place on a story. The glorious revolution. Surely you've heard of it?'

She found his mocking tone intensely irritating. 'Yes,' she said coldly. 'I've heard of it. I've also heard that both sides aren't too particular about what they shoot at.'

'That's right. It's open season on anything that moves, even American journalists.' He gave her a hard, unsmiling look. 'But I'm going to get my story, one way or another, and to do that I've got to get out of here.'

She knew there was no point in arguing with a man like this. He was the kind of person who would simply do as he pleased, regardless of his safety or anyone else's convenience. She was beginning to think that he was probably the most cynical, hard-bitten man she had ever met. What did she care if he wanted to go out and get himself killed all for the sake of a stupid story?

'Suit yourself,' she said brusquely. 'You're safe enough here, so long as you keep quiet and stay out of sight. The soldiers never come upstairs. As your doctor, I can only tell you that if you leave before your wound heals properly and you get your strength back, you'll be committing suicide.' She shrugged non-committally and gave him a cool smile. 'But it's your life.'

For the first time, she felt that she had his full attention. It was as though her off-hand little speech had made an impact on him that her earlier concern couldn't. There was an almost startled look on his face, a fleeting glance of respect, then it closed down again.

'I'll decide that later,' he said. 'You must realise, however, that my being here puts you in danger.'

'Possibly, but I'm getting used to that. Besides, they need me. I'm the only doctor within a hundred miles.'

'I'd like to clean up,' he said. He sat up a little straighter. 'Do you have a shower, or were you planning on giving me a bed-bath?'

She gave him a cold stare. 'The bathroom is right across the hall. There's a stall shower, and a razor, if you care to shave.'

He raised one dark eyebrow and once again the hard smile appeared on his face. 'All prepared for male guests, I see,' he commented.

Anger rose in Jessica like a red surge, almost blinding her. She crossed her arms in front of her and glared down at him.

'I don't know who you are or what you want,' she said icily, 'but I'd like to remind you that I saved your life last night. I rather regret that now, but I did take an oath to preserve life when I became a doctor, and I can't shake that off easily.'

'Your bedside manner is charming,' he murmured when she had finished.

She put her knuckles on the edge of the bed and leaned over him. 'No,' she said, 'it's not. It doesn't have to be. I'll let you stay here until you're well, but that's as far as my bedside manner goes.' She straightened up. 'While you're in my care, you'll follow *my* rules and do what *I* tell you to do, or you can leave right now.'

Their eyes locked together for a long moment, hers blazing with anger, his cold and appraising. Then, to her astonishment, he smiled, a real smile this time, and one that lit up his whole face.

'You're right,' he said. 'I'm sorry—I appreciate your help. I know you saved my life last night. I was out of line. My name is Jason Strong, and I'm really not a spy.'

She recognised the name immediately. His by-line had appeared in newspapers and magazines for years as a foreign correspondent from all the most dangerous trouble spots of the world: South-east Asia, the Middle East, El Salvador, Northern Ireland, the Balkans. He had written books, appeared on television, even won some kind of medal and several prizes, she recalled vaguely. She had only a very hazy recollection of what he looked like, but she never would have connected him with this gaunt, unshaven man in the bed.

'I've heard of you,' she said. 'I'm Jessica Carpenter.'

He inclined his head gravely. 'Dr Carpenter,' he said. 'Now, I really would like to clean up.' He rubbed his stubbly chin with a grimace of distaste.

'Do you think you can make it by yourself?' she asked.

He threw the blanket off and cautiously moved his legs over the edge of the bed. He was still wearing the dirty khaki trousers he had appeared in last night, and, she noticed too, the belt was still unbuckled so that they rode low on his hips.

As a doctor, of course, she had seen naked men before, but had learned early to detach herself from the individual. Now, however, the thought of those loosened trousers slipping down when he stood up gave her a brief moment's pause. It was gone as quickly as it came, but the knowing look in Jason Strong's eyes told her that he had seen it and that he knew.

Casually, he rebuckled the belt, and then slid off the bed on to his feet. Immediately, he started swaying. His face was suddenly drained of colour, and he reached out blindly for support.

She was at his side instantly, there to catch him as he slumped against her and she held him by the arms until the wave of dizziness passed. He hung his head, shook it a little, then gave her a grim look.

'You were right, Doctor. I'm weaker than I thought.'

'You'll be all right,' she said gently. 'It's good for you to move around. Just take it slow and easy. I'll help you.'

She put an arm around his waist and guided him slowly out to the hall and on into the bathroom. When she let go of him, he leaned weakly against the wall while she went to the medicine cabinet. She came back to him with a sheet of plastic wrap and some masking tape.

'You must keep the dressing dry,' she said as she taped the plastic securely over his bandage. When she was through, she looked at him. 'Do you want me to help you?'

For one second, a malicious gleam appeared in the hard grey eyes. Then he shook his head. 'No thanks. I can manage now.'

She nodded. 'Don't try to rush things. There's shaving gear in the medicine cabinet, and I'll fix you something to eat while . . .'

Just then there came a loud banging on the front door downstairs. Jessica glanced at her watch. It was almost eight. It would be Varga and his men. She darted a quick look at the suddenly tense man beside her. The cold look of suspicion was back.

'That's Varga,' she said. 'Go on. Take your shower. I'll stall him and be back in half an hour.'

CHAPTER TWO

WHILE Jessica was downstairs fobbing off Captain Varga with a story about some blood tests she had to run, Jason Strong did manage to shower and shave by himself, but when she got back upstairs, breathless from the risks she was taking, he was back in bed with his head turned away from her, apparently worn out by the effort.

She went into the kitchen and put on the coffee, then retrieved his filthy clothes from the bathroom and the room where he was sleeping. She would have to wash them out in the bathtub and hang them to dry over the towel racks. She couldn't use the ancient washer downstairs off the surgery. All she needed was to have Captain Varga come in just as she was rinsing out a very large pair of khaki trousers and shirt and men's jockey shorts.

As she prepared breakfast back up in the kitchen, she remembered that the previous tenant of the house, a Dr Brownlee from Texas, had left some ragged clothes behind when he left. She had stored them in a box, shoved them far back in the cupboard of the extra bedroom, thinking to use them later for rags, then forgotten about them. She had no idea what size Dr Brownlee had been, never having met the man, or what the condition of the old clothing might be, but it would have to be better than nothing.

She piled a tray with scrambled eggs, toast, juice and coffee, and as she carried it back to the bedroom, she felt an odd little thrill of excitement at the strange situation she found herself in. It was dangerous, she knew. If Captain Varga found out she was harbouring what he considered to be a spy in her house, he was quite capable of having them both shot.

It wasn't entirely the physical danger, however, that caused her heart to beat a little faster, her knees to feel a little weak. If Jason Strong stayed out of sight upstairs and was quiet, there was no real reason to fear for their safety. There was something about the man himself that gave her this odd off-balance sensation. On the surface, he appeared controlled, and had even had the grace to apologise to her last night for baiting her, but she still sensed real danger from him. There was far more behind those hard slate-blue eyes than he revealed, and she had already seen flashes of the carefully leashed power that was in him.

He was still sleeping. She set the tray down on the bedside table and stood looking down at him. The transformation in him from the shower and shave was astounding. He was not a handsome man in the conventional sense. His mouth was too set and thin, his nose a little too long and his cheeks too sunken for that. He had a long face with a strong chin and prominent bones. His eyebrows were heavy and dark, his thatch of black hair unruly and far too long, as though he hadn't bothered to have it cut for several weeks.

His only softening feature was the eyelashes, long and thick and coal-black, that lay on the sharply etched bones of his cheeks. Jessica's eyes moved down over the long neck, the broad shoulders and wide upper chest, all deeply tanned, hard, sinewy. He looked like an athlete, not massive like a weight-lifter or a football player, she mused, but more like a swimmer or a pole-vaulter.

Suddenly she became aware that his eyes had opened and that he was staring at her. She couldn't read what was behind the steady gaze; his expression was impenetrable. She quickly turned away and picked up the tray.

'I've brought your breakfast,' she said briefly.

Silently, Jason pulled himself up to a sitting position. The thin blanket fell loosely around his waist, revealing the rest of his smooth tanned chest, the muscled rib-cage and the beginning of his hard, flat abdomen.

'Can you manage by yourself?' she asked.

He only nodded. He picked up the glass of juice and raised it to his lips, his expression never changing, his eyes still firmly fixed on her while he drank.

She turned and went over to the closet. 'I've got your clothes soaking in the bathtub,' she called over her shoulder. 'There are some old men's clothes in here somewhere you might be able to wear.' She found the box stuck right at the back of the cupboard and pulled it out. 'I don't know if they'll fit, but you can try them on when you feel stronger.'

She carried the box over to the centre of the room and set it down on the floor. He was eating now, slowly and without much relish, and he glanced down at the box.

'Good,' he said. 'It'll have to do; I want to leave tonight right after it gets dark.'

She stood up, put her hands on her hips and walked towards the bed. 'And just how do you plan to do that in your condition?'

Totally ignoring her question, he took a swallow of coffee. 'Did you pacify Varga?'

'Yes,' she said curtly. 'Listen, you can barely walk yet. How do you expect to manage out there in the mountains by yourself?' She waved an arm in that direction.

He stared at her quizzically for a moment, then smiled. 'You're very pretty when you're angry,' he said.

She was about to utter a sharp retort, but then realised that was just what he wanted. Instead, she fought down her irritation and forced herself to smile back at him.

'And you're a very devious man,' she said. Then she shrugged and turned to go. 'It's your life. I have to get down to the surgery or Captain Varga will be banging on the door again.' At the doorway she turned. 'I have rounds to make in the village this morning, but I'll be back by noon.'

She nodded curtly at him and left.

When she finally let Captain Varga in half an hour later, he was not only very annoyed at the delay, he also seemed suspicious.

'There is an American spy in the area,' he pronounced as she stitched up a deep gash in the forehead of one of his men. 'He may come here to your house.'

'I doubt it,' she said calmly as she bandaged the soldier's wound. She looked up at Varga from her stool. 'I'm ready for the next one, then I have to go check on Mrs Morales' baby.'

The shooting had resumed again that morning. That meant more wounded for her to tend. The minute this battle is over, she had vowed to herself when she heard the familiar booming of the guns, I'm going to take Marshall's advice and get out of San Cristobal.

'Nevertheless,' Captain Varga went on, 'I will station a guard near your house just in case the American does show up. He is wounded, and may seek a doctor.'

Jessica shrugged. 'That's all right with me,' she said casually. She stood up and went to the sink to wash her hands. 'If you want to waste a soldier, that's your affair.' She turned to face him. 'But he won't come here, your spy.' She dried her hands. 'If he's got any sense, he won't come anywhere near the village.'

Varga eyed her narrowly. 'Perhaps not. I will post the guard anyway.'

She finally got rid of him and his soldiers by eleven o'clock. Then she got her bag and went outside to make her rounds, locking the door carefully behind her. She had told Jason he would be safe. She only prayed she was right.

When she finished checking on the new baby and his mother, she hurried back across the hot dusty square to her house. True to his word, Captain Varga had stationed a soldier there. He was sitting on top of the low stucco wall that surrounded the house, smoking a cigarette and holding his rifle across his lap. As she passed by him, she gave him a tight smile. He grinned back at her and waved.

The front door was still locked tightly, and after she let herself inside, she bolted it securely behind her and then slumped back against it with a sigh of relief.

Jason was sleeping when she looked in on him, but he seemed to have some sixth sense that alerted him to her presence, because when she came back a few minutes later with his lunch, he was wide awake and sitting up in bed. When she told him about the guard, to her surprise he took it quite well. He only frowned briefly, got that familiar closed-in expression on his face, apparently thinking it over, then nodded, as though he had come to an inner decision.

'That settles it, then,' he said. 'It looks like you're stuck with me for a while.'

She didn't say a word. She only set his lunch tray down on the bedside table and silently handed him a napkin.

'Won't he mind?' he said then with a jerk of his head in the direction of the box of clothing, still sitting on the floor where she had left it that morning.

She stared at him blankly. 'Won't who mind?'

'The guy the clothes belong to. And the razor.'

'They belonged to the doctor who lived here before I came. Why should he mind?'

He gave her one of his thin smiles. 'I guess he won't, then,' he said. He took the tray from her and started to eat his lunch.

She turned to leave. 'I'll go and have my own lunch, now,' she said. 'Afterwards, I'll check your arm and put a clean dressing on it.'

He didn't say anything, and when she returned to the kitchen, she wondered if she shouldn't have taken her own lunch in with his and eaten with him. No, she thought, as she sat down at the rickety table and started in on her sandwich, it's better this way; keep it on a distinctly doctor-patient basis. He was a disturbing man, and in a way she couldn't quite put her finger on, but definitely unlike any other man she had ever known before.

The trouble was, she thought as she rinsed out her dishes at the sink, he was indefinable, unfathomable, an unknown quantity. He gave away so little. He wore a well-practised mask, and even his rare smiles seemed calculated. She simply didn't know what to make of him.

But, then, she thought as she went down to the surgery to get her bag, it doesn't really matter. When the soldiers leave, he'll be gone, and I'll be going home.

He was just finishing the last of his coffee when she got back to his room. She picked up the tray and set it back on the table, then pulled the wooden chair over to the side of the bed and sat down. Silently, she set to work to remove the bandage.

'You're a woman of few words,' he said at last.

She darted him a quick glance. 'We're taught in medical school to give all our attention to our patients and concentrate only on the problem.'

She had to admit, though, as she examined the wound, that she was finding this difficult to do. She could hardly forget he was a man when everything about him was so overpoweringly male.

He slept most of the first two days he was there, and after a long and rather bitter argument that first evening, when she finally ended by threatening to turn him over to Captain Varga, he finally agreed to take a sleeping-pill at night.

The next night he was a little more docile about taking it, but only just. He was a strong-minded man, and didn't take well to obedience. She stood by the side of the bed, a determined set to her chin, holding out the pill in the palm of one hand, a glass of water in the other.

He made a face and reached for the pill. 'Would you really turn me in if I didn't take it?'

She hesitated. She wouldn't, of course, but she was wary about telling him that. 'I might as well,' she hedged, forcing the glass of water into his unwilling hand. 'You still have a slight fever. If you were to wake up in the night and start shouting or crying out, the guard outside would hear you, and we'd both be in the soup.'

'I never shout or cry out in my sleep,' he said firmly.

'I'm not going to take that chance,' she said, just as firmly. 'A sick person does all kinds of things he wouldn't do if he were well.'

'I'm not sick,' he grumbled.

She raised an eyebrow. 'No? Well, that's news to me. Just swallow the pill and let's get it over with. I've had a long day and want to get some sleep tonight for a change.'

By the third day, he felt strong enough to get up for his meals, and by evening, when she locked up the surgery for the day and came upstairs, she could see that he was getting restless as he grew stronger.

He was pacing around the living room when she got there, stopping every once in a while to examine a picture on the wall or an embroidered hanging Mrs Morales had made for her. She stood in the shadow of the upstairs landing, watching him. She knew he would insist on leaving soon, and was surprised at the small jolt of regret the thought made her feel.

The clothes fitted him passably well. The doctor had apparently been a smaller man across the shoulders and a little shorter. Jason was a few inches over six feet, she thought, tall and rangy with a well-defined muscle structure. The faded blue jeans were a little tight in the legs, and the torn cotton-knit shirt hugged his frame tightly, outlining his back and chest and rib-cage.

He turned just then and glanced her way. She

walked into the room, suddenly uncomfortable under the steady gaze. She wished again that she wasn't so intensely aware of this man. I'll be glad when he's gone, she said to herself, but knew a part of her didn't believe it for a minute.

'You look beat,' he said at last. 'Hard day?'

Jessica ran a hand over her hair and gave him a brief smile. 'No more than usual. You're looking fit.'

He was. His colour was good, and the haggard look was gone. The blue-grey eyes were still stony and secretive, but there was a spark in them now that had been missing before when he was so weak. He walked more confidently, too, and held himself well.

'Are you hungry?' she asked, moving into the adjoining kitchen.

'Why not let me make dinner?' Jason replied, walking towards her.

Jessica looked at him in surprise. 'You?'

'Sure. I haven't been a bachelor for thirty-seven years for nothing. I don't cook fancy, but it'll be edible.' When she didn't move, he put a hand lightly on her shoulder and gave her a little shove. 'Go on. Take a shower, put your feet up and relax.'

'Sounds good,' she said at last.

When she came back, half an hour later, showered and dressed in a loose caftan of pale yellow linen, her freshly washed and dried hair hanging loose about her shoulders, he was just dishing up a steaming bowl of rice and tomatoes. A tossed salad was already on the table, which was casually set with the only unchipped dishes she owned, also left by the previous tenant.

He looked up when he saw her in the doorway. He raised his dark eyebrows a fraction of an inch and stared for a few seconds. A momentary gleam flashed in his eyes, then was gone. He picked up the tomato dish and set it on the table, gesturing for her to sit down.

'This is a real treat,' she said as she filled her plate. 'I hate cooking.'

'Ah,' he said, 'a truly liberated woman.'

The way he said it, it didn't sound like much of a compliment, and she frowned. 'I don't even know what that means. I don't dislike domestic chores because I'm rebelling against traditional feminine activity, but because with my work, I don't have time for it.'

'I can relate to that,' he said, nodding. 'I feel the same way myself. Whether you're male or female, if you have work to do that absorbs all your energy and attention, it's natural to resent whatever interferes with it.' He gave her a thoughtful look. 'I wasn't trying to pigeon-hole you or lump you into a category.'

They ate in silence after that, and when he had finished, he pushed his plate away and leaned back with a sigh of contentment.

'This is very good,' Jessica said, helping herself to another small serving. She nodded at his empty plate. 'I'm glad to see you've got your appetite back. You're looking much better.'

'I feel better, too, but I'd give a lot for a cigarette right now,' he said a little wistfully.

She laughed. 'Sorry. I don't smoke, and Captain Varga knows it. Even if I could get you some cigarettes, he'd smell it in a minute. He's a very suspicious man.'

'Especially of American spies.' He leaned forward and propped his elbows on the table. 'Speaking of that, since I don't know when I'll be able to get out of here, I'd at least like to get some work done. Do you have any writing materials I could use? Anything will do. I've composed my copy on the backs of envelopes and the margins of old newspapers when I couldn't get something better.'

'Of course,' she said, rising from her chair.

'Not now. Tomorrow will do. Sit down. I made some coffee.' She sat back down and let him wait on her. It was very pleasant, she thought, not to have to do everything herself. He was a very unusual man, apparently secure enough in his own masculinity not to resent serving a woman or doing menial domestic tasks.

'Tell me about yourself,' he said when he had poured their coffee. 'What's a beautiful young doctor doing in the wilds of San Crístobal during a revolution?'

'Well, there wasn't a revolution when I first came here a year ago.' She took a sip of coffee. 'I'm not sure now why I did come. I was fresh out of my internship and wanted to do something useful, something besides setting myself up in a dull, lucrative practice in Virginia, anyway.'

'That's where you're from? Virginia?'

She nodded. 'Yes, the northern part, a small town near Washington just across the Maryland border.'

'Beautiful country,' he commented. 'I'm very fond of Virginia. I live in Washington when I'm in the States. Do you have family there?'

'Only a brother. He teaches at Georgetown University in Washington. Our parents died when I was just a little girl. Charles is quite a bit older than I am, almost fifteen years, and he and his wife brought me up.'

He stared at her for a moment. 'Charles Carpenter

is your brother?'

'Yes. Do you know him?'

'Just slightly.' His eyes travelled over her. 'I don't see much family resemblance.'

She laughed. 'No one does. We take after different sides of the family.'

He seemed to be about to say something, then changed his mind. He sat drinking his coffee in silence for a while, then said, 'What will you do now? When you leave here?'

'Go back to Virginia, I suppose.'

'And set up that lucrative practice? You don't sound very enthusiastic about the prospect.'

She shrugged. 'It's sounding better and better to me after my year here. I think I've had my fill of revolution.' She eyed him over her coffee cup. 'How about you? What are your plans?'

He got up and took his cup to the counter to refill it, standing with his back to her. 'Oh, me—I never plan ahead. I just go where the stories are. When I finish up here, I'll probably head for Poland.' He came back to the table and stood over her, smiling the familiar tight, dry smile. 'Or possibly Afghanistan.'

She looked up at him. His expression was unreadable. He had that closed-in look again. She smiled thinly.

'Wherever there's trouble,' she said. 'You really like danger.'

He thought this over for a few seconds, sipping slowly on his coffee. Then he nodded. 'I've never thought of it in quite those terms, but, yes, you're probably right.'

In the next two days, they established a routine of daily life that kept them pretty much out of each other's way. She still insisted that he take the sleeping pill every night, and he still argued with her, but in the end, perhaps to set her real fears for their safety at rest, he ended by swallowing it.

She was as busy as ever with her medical duties, both for the soldiers and the villagers, so was gone all day and sometimes much of the night. She found him the writing materials he asked for, and whenever she was home, he seemed to be bent over the kitchen table scribbling on the yellow legal pad she had unearthed.

He continued to cook their evening meal from the supply of canned goods she had stocked in the cupboard. There was still fresh fruit and vegetables to be had at the market stall in the village, and even an occasional loaf of home-baked bread or a chicken, given to her in payment for her services.

The gunfire continued throughout the day, and the bored sentry was still posted day and night outside Jessica's house. By now, she had become accustomed to the whole odd situation so that it had even come to seem quite normal to her, and gradually, her fears diminished.

She realised, too, that it helped her morale in some inexplicable way to have Jason Strong living in the house with her. His solid, confident and mainly silent presence reassured her, made her feel safer somehow, as though she were not really so alone in this alien country any more.

Their conversation at dinner, the one meal they shared, remained casual, barely skirting the personal, and she learned little more about him. He would give her bare facts when she asked him about his background or his work, but she never came close to the real man. She learned that his parents had been divorced for years, and that he didn't hold either of them, nor the married state in general, in high esteem. He was, simply, a loner, who gave away nothing of his true feelings, and there were times, especially when he was speaking of his parents, when a cruel twist would appear on the thin mouth that almost frightened her.

He was a hard man, she thought, as she watched him bending over his writing, totally absorbed in his work, or when the deep eyes would glaze over when he spoke of his mother's fourth husband. But she also found him oddly compelling. He was so self-contained, so inward, and, she had to admit, so physically appealing, that she longed to find a way to penetrate that cast-iron surface of his. His eyes especially fascinated her. They seemed to change colour almost at will, going from a sparkling blue when he smiled openly, to a dull slate colour when he hid behind them. When he was especially tired, they turned a grey shade that reminded her of winter rain.

There were times, too, when she sat under the lamplight at night darning his torn clothes or reading over her daily charts and he was working at the table, that she could swear he was staring at her. This generated a strange aura of tension in the very air, which, combined with the gunfire, the guard outside, put her in an almost constant state of contained excitement, as though she were waiting for something to happen—something important.

Once or twice, when she felt his eyes on her like that in the evening, she was strongly tempted to look up from her task to find out if they really were. But she never did. It was as though she was afraid of what she might see there.

He'll be gone soon, anyway, she told herself at

those times, and I'll be going back to Virginia myself before long. We'll probably never see each other again, and I'll look back on this whole episode as merely an interesting experience of no real importance.

Nevertheless, on the fourth day of his stay, as she was walking home early in the evening from her rounds, she realised with a sudden jolt that Jason Strong was the main thing on her mind these days. She hardly noticed the gunfire any more, and the soldiers' presence no longer gave her the uneasy feeling it had at first.

A storm was brewing in the nearby mountains, giving the trees a sickly greenish cast and darkening the sky with thunderclouds. Those sudden storms closed in quickly. Already she could see lightning flashes in the distance and hear the muffled claps of thunder as they approached the village. She quickened her step to get home before it broke.

As she hurried across the deserted square toward the house, her heart automatically picked up its beat at the thought that she would be seeing him in a few minutes. In a way, she thought as she swung open the gate and started up the path, it will be better when he does go and I can get my mind back on other things. But at the same time, her spirits sank at the prospect.

She went inside the house, bolting the heavy door carefully behind her, and ran lightly up the stairs to the living quarters. On the landing she could already smell the food cooking in the kitchen, and she was filled with pleasurable anticipation at another evening ahead spent in his company.

He was sitting at the kitchen table writing and hadn't heard her come in over the noise of the storm outside. She set her black bag down and stood in the doorway looking in at him, bent over his work. He had on one of the thin cotton knit shirts that left his arms bare, and from time to time he would reach over and rub a hand over his bandaged wound, as though it itched.

His face was in profile to her, the eyes downcast, and she simply stared, glad of the chance to watch him unobserved. She thought he had the most interesting face she had ever seen. He was frowning slightly, concentrating and totally absorbed in his work, a lock of the too-long black hair falling over his forehead, his pencil tapping lightly on the legal pad as he groped for a word or a phrase.

Then he smiled, a secret, inward smile, as he apparently found what he was looking for, and began furiously scribbling on the pad. She still stood there, rooted to the spot, staring, unable to tear her eyes away from him. He was hunched further over the table as he wrote, so that the ill-fitting shirt rode up high at the back over the waistband of his faded jeans, revealing several inches of smooth tanned back.

Suddenly, his hand stilled, and at the same time his eyes darted sideways to look directly into hers. There wasn't time for her to shift her gaze, and although she was flustered at being caught out staring at him, a strange compulsion held her there motionless.

A glowing warmth filled her, and she knew her cheeks must be flaming by now. Still she couldn't move. Dimly, she heard the storm, moving in fast now, and the whistling wind that always preceded it, but the electric tension that crackled in the air between them was not only from the storm.

There came a great clap of thunder then. It sounded as though it was directly overhead, and she cried out in alarm, the spell between them broken. She had been in many similar storms before, but never one that came quite this close or caught her in such a vulnerable moment.

In the next second he was out of his chair and standing before her, gripping her by the arms. 'Jess, are you all right?' he asked with concern.

At his firm touch on her bare arms she came to her senses. She stared at him wide-eyed for a moment, then dropped her gaze and gave a little laugh.

'Yes, of course. I don't know what got into me. I'm not usually bothered by thunder.' She laughed again nervously. 'It must be the soldiers, the guns, the whole odd situation.'

He nodded, but made no move to release his hold on her. His touch felt like fire on her skin. If I move a fraction of an inch toward him, she thought with a sudden instinctive certainty, I'll end up in his arms. Is that what I want?

In the split second that followed, she made her decision. Of course it was what she wanted, she knew, but then what? She had trained herself not to act impulsively, to choose a course and then stay on it. She never would have made it through medical school without that kind of single-minded perseverance.

She gently disengaged herself from his grasp and averted her eyes. His hands dropped instantly to his sides, as she knew they would at the slightest suggestion of withdrawal on her part. He was a determined man, but she was certain he would never force himself on a woman.

'Dinner smells good,' she said lightly, walking over to the stove and lifting the lid off the simmering pot. She sniffed at it, then replaced the lid and half turned in his direction, not quite facing him nor meeting his eyes. 'You're going to spoil me. What shall I do when you're gone and I have to cook my own supper again?'

'I'm sure you'll manage quite well,' he said in an even tone, 'a self-reliant girl like you.'

He understood immediately, of course, as she knew he would, that her comment actually pertained to something far more significant than food. In the swift by-play, she had made it clear that she couldn't afford an involvement with him, and he had bowed gracefully to her decision.

Lying in bed later that night, however, she wondered if she had made the right decision. Every day that he was there she grew more attracted to him, and now she knew that he felt the same way.

What would have happened, she wondered, if she had taken that small step toward him? A great ache of longing gripped her as she considered the consequences. It would be heaven, she knew, to be held in those strong arms, to feel that thin, mobile mouth on hers, to be pressed up against that long, lithe body.

But then what? As soon as he could, he would be gone. She knew that as a certainty. She didn't know him very well, she realised, and he kept a good part of himself hidden, but she did know that he was not the kind of man to stay in one place long or settle for a steady, dull life.

I did the right thing tonight, she thought, as she shifted her position in bed for the tenth time. When the fighting stops, he'll leave, and I'll never see him again.

CHAPTER THREE

THE next day, they went on as they had before the night of the storm, each busy with his own work, his own thoughts, but there was a distinct increase in the tension between them. They were elaborately polite to each other over the evening meal, speaking only of inconsequential matters, and in the most distant, impersonal tones.

After dinner, as they carried their dishes to the sink and washed up, they both seemed to go out of their way to avoid any possibility of physical contact. While Jason was at the sink rinsing out dishes, Jessica put food away in the small refrigerator on the opposite side of the room, and they worked silently, as though they had both run out of trivia to discuss and just decided to give up trying to find a safe subject.

When they were through, Jessica announced that she was going downstairs to work on her charts. In response, Jason only nodded, apparently relieved to get her out of the way, and made no comment on the fact that for the past several nights she had worked upstairs in the living-room with him.

The following day was a little better. In the afternoon, after she had finished with the soldiers, one of the Morales children came running into the surgery to announce that her mother was having pains. It turned out to be a false alarm, but Jessica stayed with her until after dark, deliberately prolonging her stay so that she wouldn't have to go home and face another strained dinner with Jason.

When she finally got home, he had already gone to his room. He had left a stew simmering low on the stove for her supper, and after she had eaten, she showered quickly and got ready for bed.

When she turned out the hall light, she noticed a crack of yellow glow coming from underneath his door. He must be reading or working in bed, she thought, and hoped he had remembered to take his sleeping pill. Although he was recovering nicely from his wound and had no more fever, he was still weaker than he realised from all the blood he had lost and the energy expended on the healing process. She knew from experience that people in that condition slept more deeply than they would normally, and there was a real danger of night sweats, bad dreams and crying out involuntarily. With the guard diligently patrolling the front of the house, they couldn't afford to take that chance.

She hesitated at the door to his room, remembering their nightly battles over the sleeping pill she insisted he take and which he stubbornly resisted. Should she knock and remind him? She wouldn't even have to open the door, she could just call out to him.

Finally, she decided against it. He had been all right last night, and somehow, at the moment, standing in the hall in her nightgown and knowing he was lying naked in his bed just on the other side of the door, she felt it was far less dangerous to risk alerting the sentry to his presence in the house than it did to face another tense confrontation with him. She turned and walked quietly down the hall to her own room and went to bed.

Much later, she was awakened out of a sound sleep by a strange noise. She sat bolt upright in bed, only half awake and filled with a sudden fear. Was the gunfire coming closer? Was another storm on the way? Calming herself, she listened and it came again. It seemed to be something inside the house.

Then she realized that it was the sound of a man's hoarse cries. '*Damn* that stubborn idiot!' she muttered as she swung her legs over the side of the bed. The one night she hadn't stood over him to make sure, he hadn't taken his sleeping pill and was having a nightmare. As she ran barefoot down the hall to his room, she grew angrier with each step. She had to get to him and wake him up before the guard heard him.

It was just like a man, she seethed, always to think he knew best. She had warned him and warned him, but no, he was going to do what he wanted to do regardless of their safety. She flipped on the hall light, threw his door open and rushed over to the side of the bed. He was still crying out and tossing his head to and fro on the pillows. The thin blanket had become disarranged in his struggles and was tangled around his waist.

She sat down on the edge of the bed and leaned over him, shaking him. The skin of his chest and shoulders was a little damp, and she felt the powerful muscles tense and stiffen under her touch.

'Jason,' she hissed, bending her face close to his, her mouth at his ear. She shook him again. 'Jason, do you hear me? Wake up! For God's sake, wake up!'

Then, suddenly, he was still. He lay there quietly for a moment. She sat back and watched him. He blinked a few times, then opened his eyes and propped himself up on his elbows, staring at her. The dim light spilling in from the hall cast a shadow over the lower half of his face, highlighting the deep eyes, hooded now as he came slowly awake, and sharply etching the prominent cheekbones. His thick dark hair was even more unruly than usual.

'What is it?' he murmured groggily. 'What's happened?'

'You were having a nightmare,' she whispered. 'I was afraid the guard would hear you.'

Still angry, she was about to accuse him of not following her orders and taking his pill when something in his eyes stopped her. He was staring fixedly at her, first into her eyes, then dropping lower, and it suddenly occurred to her that all she had on was a thin cotton nightgown. She had been so anxious to get to him to quieten him that she hadn't even thought to put on a robe.

She drew in her breath sharply as the dark gaze bored into her. A very warm, not at all unpleasant glow was beginning to steal through her, and she edged away from him.

'I—I'd better go,' she said, and started to rise.

He sat up, then, the blanket slipping lower around his hips to reveal the hard stomach and the fine line of hair that tapered down from his waist. His arm shot out and he took her by the hand.

'No,' he said thickly. 'Don't go, Jessica. Stay with me.'

She couldn't speak, couldn't look at him. His hand slid up her arm to rest on her bare shoulder. It felt large and warm and strong, and she shivered under the touch. He was pulling her gently, urging her toward him now. She could smell the harsh clean soap on his skin as he came closer. She knew she should get up right now and go back to her own room, but it was as though she was held there by some powerful force against her will.

It was inevitable, she thought in a sudden brief

flash of insight. This is what we've been building up to ever since he came. His other hand came to rest at the base of her throat for a moment or two, then his fingers lightly traced the line of her collar bone, hesitating at the strap of her nightgown.

'Jessica?' he murmured.

She knew what he was asking. She forced herself to meet his gaze. The sleepy, hooded eyes were enquiring, but not supplicating. It was her choice. She could leave right now and no harm would be done. They would go on as before.

Barely, almost imperceptibly, she nodded, and watched as he rose up further out of the bed and lowered his head toward her. She raised her face to his. He gave her one last look, then closed his eyes, and his mouth came down on hers.

She had never been kissed in quite that way before. His mouth had opened before claiming hers, then closed again over her lips in a gentle, highly sensual pulling motion that left her weak and panting for more. The next time, he left his mouth open, keeping it pressed tightly against hers and forcing his darting tongue past her lips, seeking and penetrating deep inside.

When at last he lifted his head, he looked down at her, his hands still on her shoulders, his breath coming in short gasps.

'God, how I've wanted you, Jess,' he said in a strangled voice that seemed to be wrenched out of his throat. His hands were kneading her shoulders, and she felt as though her bones had all turned to rubber, totally pliable and responsive under his touch.

'I've watched you,' he went on in a low voice, 'ached for you, ever since I came here. So competent, so stern, so cool. And so beautiful.'

His right hand slid slowly downward now until she felt it resting, trembling slightly, on her breast. He just let it lie there for a few moments, perfectly still, as though silently staking his claim on her body.

His near-black eyes bored into hers, asking another question. She still couldn't speak. Her tongue felt thick in her mouth, and there was a choking sensation in her throat. She could only nod weakly and watch while he moved both hands to the thin straps of her nightgown and slipped them slowly off her shoulders.

He gazed down at her for a long time, then raised his eyes to hers again.

'You're exactly the way I knew you'd be,' he murmured. 'Full and ripe, every inch a desirable woman.'

He cupped one breast in his hand and lowered his mouth to taste the soft tender flesh, little nipping kisses, until his lips parted to take the thrusting tip inside. While his mouth and tongue performed their magic on her breast, his other hand slid the nightgown lower, pulling her up so that he could slide it down over her hips.

With a low groan, he raised his head and kissed her again, his hands travelling feverishly over every inch of her bare body. He was on his knees now, the blanket falling away entirely, and pressing himself up against her with one hand on her hips, pulling her close.

'Touch me,' he muttered into her ear. 'Show me you want me, too.'

She had touched his bare skin before, of course, the night he first came and she had undressed him and tended his wound, but it had been different then, nothing like it was now. Even though she had admired his lean strength from the first time she had seen him, her manner had been detached and professional.

Now, that seemed like another lifetime, as though they were two different people. The muscles of his back and shoulders were firm and hard as she slid her hands over them now, and when she allowed her fingers to flutter on his chest and over his stomach, she could feel him quivering at the touch.

Finally, he groaned and put his arms around her. He sank back down on the bed, pulling her on top of him so that they lay tightly clasped together along the full length of their bodies. She raised her head and looked down at him, her fingers trailing through the thick black hair.

'Kiss me,' he said.

As she pressed her lips eagerly to his, he rolled over on his side, taking her with him, his long hair-roughened legs nudging her on to her back. Propped up on one elbow and with his hot mouth devouring her, he moved his free hand feverishly up and down her body, until she reached such a pitch of longing that she dug her fingernails into his back.

She tore her mouth from his and murmured breathlessly into his ear, 'Oh, please, Jason! Now! Please!'

He slid his body on top of hers then, and for the first time in her life, Jessica knew what it was to respond to a man and to be possessed by him completely.

Some time later, they lay side by side under the thin blanket. Jessica felt utterly spent, utterly satisfied and filled with a deep contentment. Jason had held her tenderly in his arms for a long time before he left her, until the last ecstatic spasm had passed and she was breathing quietly again.

She could still feel the length of him beside her in the bed and hear his slow steady breathing. She wondered if he was asleep. Although she felt drained and content, she wasn't in the least sleepy. She wanted to stay awake forever, she thought, to savour again and again the perfection of their lovemaking.

Then he spoke. 'You haven't had an awful lot of experience at this kind of thing, have you, Jess?' His voice was kind, but with a slight undertone of amusement.

'No, not a lot,' she admitted. 'A few fumbling fiascos in college when I stupidly believed it was expected of me and that meant absolutely nothing. After that, I was far too busy during the years of my medical training to have much time for romance.' She hesitated, then asked, 'Did I disappoint you?'

'Oh, no, Jess, you didn't disappoint me. Far from it. You were everything I'd hoped you'd be: warm, responsive, giving.'

He shifted so that he was facing her and raised himself up on one elbow to prop his head in his hand. He reached out to run two fingers along her mouth, then over her chin, her throat, the valley between her breasts. Jessica shivered a little at the sensations aroused in her by his touch. Finally, the hand settled at her waist.

'How do you mean?' he teased. ' "Fumbling fiascos." '

'Well,' she said smiling up at him, 'I don't want to make you any more conceited than you probably already are, but you and those two fraternity boys that make up my lurid past could belong to two different species.'

'I'll take that as a compliment,' he said, kissing her lightly on the nose.

'You should.' She laughed. 'I was convinced I was frigid, as a matter of fact, until you came along. That's how wonderful those two were.'

'Well, you know what they say. There are no frigid women, only insensitive men.'

'You made that up,' she accused lightly. 'But you might be right.'

The hand on her waist started travelling, and to her amazement, she felt desire rising up in her again. He threw one leg over hers, and when she felt his hard thigh pressing against her, she knew the same thing was happening to him.

'Since the first act turned out so well,' he murmured against her mouth, 'shall we try for an encore?'

The days that followed were the happiest Jessica had ever known. She floated through her daily chores on a cloud, so filled with the pleasure Jason gave her that she lived in a constant state of euphoria.

All her anxiety about the revolution, the presence of the soldiers, the danger they were in, was forgotten. The constant gunfire no longer made her nervous, even when it seemed to be coming closer. In fact, she almost welcomed it, because it meant he would stay, and she now viewed the sentry still stationed outside her house with a positively benevolent glow.

Nagging at the back of her mind, however, was the knowledge that he would leave, ultimately. She had made up her mind firmly right from the beginning of their affair that she would not look ahead or try to predict the future, or even to wonder if they would have a future. He never spoke of it, and neither did she, but she couldn't help nursing the hope that somehow, when all this was over and they were both back in the States, they would at least continue to see each other.

After all, he had said he lived in Washington, and she would be in Virginia, just a few miles away. As soon as the fighting was over she would write to her father's old friend in Taunton, her home town, telling him she wanted to accept his long-standing offer of sharing his thriving medical practice with him when she came back.

Her plan, then, was to say nothing to Jason about the future until he left. He seemed to be happy with her, as pleased and satisfied with their lovemaking as she was, but she also knew it was not enough for him, that he would go as soon as he safely could, that he was anxious to get back to his work. She would wait, she decided, until then, and just as they were saying goodbye, she would casually mention the hope that they would see each other again, maybe even give him Dr Weatherby's address in Taunton. For now, though, she would keep silent and enjoy what they had.

Jessica knew, of course, just two days after their first night together, that she was madly, totally in love with him. She had no idea how he felt about her. His desire for her was unmistakable, and she knew he liked her, but not one word of love was ever spoken between them, not even at the height of their passion.

He was such a private man, she thought, as she lay beside his sleeping form late that night, and so unpredictable. She never really knew what he was thinking or feeling. This kept her constantly off-guard, but that only seemed to enhance her enchanted state. One minute he would be deeply engrossed in his writing and wouldn't even look up when she entered the room. The next, he would act as though he could never get enough of her.

Only yesterday evening, the very day after they had made such passionate love all night and slept in each other's arms for the first time, she had experienced this distancing quality in him. When she had come home late after a long day of missing him and looking forward to feeling his arms around her again, he had been at the kitchen table bent over his yellow legal pad, scribbling away. A pot of beans was simmering on the stove for their supper, but he hadn't acknowledged her presence by so much as a glance.

Hurt at the way he shut her out, she had gone down the hall to shower and change her clothes. Later, while she was standing at her dresser brushing out her long honey-coloured hair, he had come up behind her, so silently that she didn't know he was there until she caught sight of his reflection in the mirror.

Their eyes had met in the glass, but neither of them said a word. There was a look of such serious intensity on his face that all she could do was stare into those dark, slate-coloured eyes, glowing now with a contained, smouldering passion. He had put his arms around her, then, crossing them in front of her to touch her breasts under the thin blouse, his eyes never leaving hers.

By then, she could scarcely breathe from the pent-up electric tension. She could feel his body, hard and full, pressing against her from behind, but still he hadn't spoken. Then, he very slowly unfastened her blouse, button by button. When he was done, he pulled it apart and let his fingers play lightly with her throbbing, erect nipples. Watching him fondle her breasts in the mirror had aroused her so erotically that it became too painful to bear in only a few seconds.

She had groaned aloud, then, and whirled around, tearing at his clothes, clutching at him everywhere. They had stumbled to the bed and made love, quickly, impatiently, the dinner simmering on the stove in the kitchen forgotten.

They went on this way for a week. His wound was all healed now, and one night she removed the stitches. She had washed and mended the clothes he came in, but he still wore the faded jeans and shabby knitted shirts from the box in the cupboard. He looked better and stronger every day, and Jessica could see that he was growing restless in his confinement.

She didn't blame him. It couldn't be much fun for such an active man to be cooped up like that for days in a strange house, with none of his own belongings around and nowhere he could safely be seen. He had finished his story, and now when she came home in the evening he would be prowling restlessly around the living-room, like a caged animal or a small boy kept inside on a rainy day.

There was nothing she could do for him except to be there when he wanted her. Their lovemaking had become even more intense. There was a frantic, almost frenzied aspect to the way his hands explored her body, the way he thrust into her, that she knew was related to his growing impatience to be free.

And still, he hadn't mentioned how he felt about her, hadn't even said he hoped to see her again. He lived entirely in the present moment. The future apparently didn't exist for him. He never talked about next week or next month or even tomorrow.

One night, as they lay side by side in the bed, exhausted and sated, she decided she could keep silent no longer. She had begun to feel slightly used, as though she was only an object to him on which to vent his frustration. Her body was sore from his violent lovemaking, and even though at the time she had met him joyously in total surrender, now, in the aftermath, she felt just a little cheapened by his attitude toward her.

She gathered all her courage and turned her head toward him. 'Why have you never married, Jason?' she said into the darkness.

He was silent for so long that she would have thought he was asleep except that she could feel his body tense beside her. Finally, he gave a short harsh laugh.

'Why do women always manage to end up on that subject?' he said in a bitter accusing tone.

Humiliation and rage flooded through her in hot waves. She moved away from him instinctively, her body running first hot with anger, then cold with despair. She didn't dare speak. She knew she would end by either defending herself or accusing him, and either would be a mistake. She willed herself to keep silent, to breathe slowly and evenly, to fight down the unpleasant emotions rising up in her.

'I was only curious,' she said lightly, when she could speak. She tried hard to make her voice casual and pleasant, even cheerful. 'That wasn't a prelude to a proposal.' She yawned audibly and turned her back to him. 'Good night, Jason,' she said.

She felt him curl his long body against her then, and his arm came around her waist. He brushed the hair away from her face and raised himself up slightly to place his lips at her ear.

'I'm sorry, Jess,' he muttered. 'That was a stupid thing to say. I know you're not like that.' He continued to stroke her long hair. 'It's this damned confinement—it makes me edgy. I was wrong to take it out on you.' He pressed his lips to her cheek. 'Forgive me,' he murmured.

She turned in his arms and laid her head back on the pillow. 'Of course; there's nothing to forgive. I know how hard this has been on you. It can't last much longer, though, and then you can go.'

He kissed her on the mouth, a gentle, almost loving kiss. 'I knew you'd understand. You're quite a lady, Doctor.' He lay back and idly ran his hand up and down from her shoulder to her breast. 'I think you already know the answer to your question anyway,' he said sleepily. 'Marriage means a home, children. That's something I never had. All my father was interested in was making money, and my mother was so anxious to keep herself attractive to the latest in her long string of men, that neither one of them cared anything about making a home. As a consequence, I wouldn't even know where to start. I spent my whole childhood with a series of housekeepers or tucked safely out of sight in boarding schools. What would I know about family life?'

Although she was still hurt, her heart went out to him. Even though her parents had died when she was very young, her much older brother and his wife, childless, had welcomed her into their home gladly and lovingly. The thought of a sensitive young boy, neglected and lonely, left in the care of strangers, made her heart ache for him.

She put her hand over his, stilling it on her breast as though to warm and comfort him, and turned her head to press her mouth to his shoulder, tasting the sweetness of his bare flesh. Everything in her longed to tell him of her love, but she knew it would be a mistake. If they were going to have any kind of future, it would have to be on his terms.

CHAPTER FOUR

THE next morning, Jessica awoke to an unfamiliar silence. The shooting had stopped during the night. In the distance a dog barked, but that was all.

She jumped out of bed, threw on a robe and ran downstairs to the surgery window that overlooked the square. It was empty. The soldiers were gone, leaving only the charred remains of their campfire. Just across the square in front of the church, she could see the local priest appear at the gate, the first time she had even seen him in two weeks.

Then, little by little, as she watched, the people of the village began creeping tentatively out into the square, first the men, then, following behind them at a distance, the braver of the young boys. The leader of the men walked over to the abandoned campfire and scuffed the toes of his boot into the dead coals.

Then he spat contemptuously in the dust and turned to beckon the others forward. Mothers with babies in their arms, old people, toddlers and children, all came swarming out of their huts into the square. Soon she heard laughter and the cries of children as they began running and jumping, overjoyed to resume their carefree games once again.

She saw a group of men settle themselves in a row on the long wooden bench under a banana tree. A bottle of wine was produced and passed around. The women stood in a huddle nearby, gossiping and watching the children at their play.

It must be over, she thought—at least, this

particular battle. Her thoughts were in a turmoil. She was relieved, of course. Now there would be no more fighting, no more killing. The village could return to its normal, dull routine. The men would go back to work at the coffee plantation, she would have no more soldiers to stitch and bandage. And Jason could leave.

She turned and went back upstairs, her conflicting emotions warring within her. There was nothing she could do. She paused at the bedroom door and looked inside. Jason was still sleeping, the covers down around his lean hips, one arm flung over his dark head, the taut, sinewy muscles of his shoulders and arms relaxed.

Maybe he won't leave right away, she thought. At least now he could go outside and move about freely. With the soldiers gone, he wouldn't have to hide in the house any more. That might satisfy him for a week or two. She decided to delay telling him. He would find out soon enough. For now, she would let him sleep.

She showered and dressed quickly. When she was through, she looked in on him again, impelled by her fears of losing him to satisfy herself that he was still there. The sight of his long body, just as she had left him before, reassured her. He hadn't even changed position. Since they had had to keep the window so heavily curtained, the room was dim, even though the morning sun was shining brightly.

Then she heard the sound of a motor and tyres crunching on the gravelled road just outside the house. She ran downstairs and unbolted the front door. When she went out on the porch, blinking and shading her eyes from the glare of the sun, she saw Marshall Bennett just getting out of his jeep.

'Marshall!' she called, and ran down the path to meet him. 'Is it really over?'

He came towards her with a wide grin of relief on his face and held his arms out to her.

'God, am I glad to see you safe!' he said, holding her tightly. 'I've been so worried about you.' He kept one arm around her shoulder and started walking toward the house. 'I couldn't get up here through the fighting, and I just kept hoping they'd need your medical skill badly enough to keep you safe.'

'Is it over, then?' she asked again. 'The revolution?'

'Hell, no,' he said disgustedly as they went inside. 'It's just moved back up into the hills.' He turned to face her. He put his hands on her shoulders and gave her a stern serious look. 'You've got to get out of here right away. There's no telling when they might come back. Planes are still leaving from the capital, and I can get you on one, but we've got to move fast. How soon can you leave.?'

Jessica's head whirled. 'I don't know, Marshall,' she stammered. 'A week? I've still got patients in the village who need my attention.'

'A week might be too late,' he said firmly. 'Make it two days. Today's Tuesday. I'll be back up on Thursday, and I want you packed and ready to leave.'

'Two days!' she murmured. She shook her head. What about Jason? Should she tell Marshall he was there with her? Maybe he could get them both out. They could leave together. Or maybe they could both stay.

She would do that, she decided. She would leave it to Jason. If he wanted to stay in San Cristobal to cover the revolution, she would stay, too. At least that way she would see him once in a while, even if he did leave the village. And if he wanted to go back to the States, Marshall could get him on a plane, too.

For now, though, she decided, she would say nothing to Marshall about it. She would agree to his plan, and when he came back on Thursday, she would either be all ready to leave with Jason, or she would tell him she was staying. She would be safe enough. Neither side would harm her, even if they should come back.

'All right, Marshall,' she said at last. 'I'll be ready. Can I fix you some breakfast?'

He shook his head and put his hand on the door. 'No. I've got to get back to the capital. We're trying to get all the Americans evacuated, just in case.' He smiled. 'Both sides are still convinced we're all spies.'

When he was gone, she ran back upstairs and saw Jason standing at the top looking down at her. He was dressed in the faded blue jeans, his chest and shoulders bare, and Jessica's heart caught in her throat at the sight of him, so tall, so strong, so necessary to her now.

'You heard?' she asked when she reached him.

He nodded gravely. 'They've gone.'

'It's still not over,' she said hurriedly. 'Marshall said the fighting had moved into the hills, but they could come back any time.' She paused, then made up her mind to tell him everything. 'Marshall is coming back the day after tomorrow. He wants me to leave the country, go back to the States.'

He nodded. 'I think that's wise.'

'You could come with me,' she blurted. 'He can get us both on a plane.'

He cocked his head to one side and gave her a thin smile. 'We'll see.'

She knew that was all she would get out of him

now. She didn't dare question him further or tell him that if he decided to stay, she would, too.

'We'll talk about it tonight,' she said, and turned to go back downstairs. 'I'm going to have a busy day. Now that the soldiers are gone, I can move more freely in the village, and there are several patients I should check on.' She smiled up at him. 'I'll be starving tonight when I get back. Cook me a good dinner.'

He smiled back at her and raised his hand in a salute.

By nightfall, Jessica was so exhausted she could barely drag herself back home. Really, she thought, as she trudged across the square carrying her bag, if I do stay I'm going to have to get a car. Even a bicycle would do. Some of the villagers lived more than a mile away out in the foothills, and she was hot, dirty, tired and hungry from her long day of rounds.

Only the thought of going home to Jason cheered her. First a shower, she thought, as she unlocked the front door, then a good dinner, and then . . . Ah, and then, another night with the man she loved.

The house seemed unnaturally quiet to her when she got inside, but then she had become accustomed to the constant sound of the guns. She shut the door behind her. No need to bolt it now with the soldiers gone and the fighting over. Besides, now that it was safe for him, Jason might have gone out into the village. There was a telephone at the church across the square, and she knew he was anxious to get his story in to the wire service at the capital.

She went upstairs. There was no sign of a meal on the kitchen stove. Usually when she came home at night after her rounds in the village, the smell of the spicy stews and bean dishes Jason prepared from the stock of cans in the cupboard would greet her the minute she had climbed to the landing of the upper floor.

The kitchen looked very neat, she thought. The round wooden table where Jason did his writing was wiped clean, the small counter and sink appeared to be freshly scrubbed, and the cracked linoleum floor shone with a recent mopping.

He was a very neat man, she thought with a sudden surge of affection for him warming her, probably because he had learned to travel so light in his work. The fewer possessions you had, the less there was to take care of.

She would give him a piece of her mind, however, she thought as she went down the hallway to her bedroom, for not having dinner ready for her when she came home. In her own room, which she hadn't slept in for the past week, she got undressed and put on a robe. On her way to the bathroom, she glanced briefly inside his bedroom. The bed was neatly made, but he wasn't there. By the time she finished showering, he would probably be back.

She wished, a little wistfully, that she had something sexy to put on for him, to surprise him. Not that it was necessary. She glowed inside at the remembrance of the hungry light that would appear in the slate-blue eyes no matter what she wore; the chemistry between them was extraordinary. All it took was a look across the table during a meal, or the slightest physical contact as they worked together in the kitchen, and the same madness would grip them both.

Just looking at him, she mused dreamily as she stood under the shower, was enough to send her into a transport of desire. She loved everything about the way he looked. The fine, lithe body, known as well to her now as her own. The large competent hands, lightly sprinkled on the backs with dark silky hair, that knew all the secrets of her own body. Even the blank, detached look that would glaze his eyes whenever he withdrew mentally from her was a source of fascination. She knew that at another time, the cold eyes would flame with desire—desire for her, she added with a satisfied smile.

After she had dressed in her white caftan and combed out her hair, she went looking for him again, but there was still no sign of him anywhere in the house. A tiny seed of anxiety began to nag at her. Could he have gone out exploring and wandered into a band of revolutionaries? She had a sudden vision of him lying wounded and bleeding out in those dry desolate foothills. Maybe even dead!

'Oh, no!' she cried aloud, clutching at her throat. I can't lose him, she prayed silently, not now that I've found him at last.

She would just have to go out looking for him, she decided. It was quite dark by now. She would get some of the village men to help her. Better change her clothes first. Then she went into his room and switched on the light. If she could tell what he was wearing when he left, it might give her a clue.

Then she saw it. Lying on the pillow of the neatly made bed was a folded square of the yellow paper he used for his writing. She stumbled across the room, snatched it up, and sat down, trembling, on the edge of the bed. A terrible dread clutched at her heart, but still she hoped.

She tore open the note. It was brief, only a few lines in his neat, print-like handwriting.

'Jess,

It's safe for me to leave now. Thanks for everything. I'll never forget you, but it's better this way.

Jason'

She read it five times, hardly able to believe it. Finally, she had to believe it. He had simply left, without even saying goodbye to her. How could he? How could anyone do such a thing to someone he had been so close to, someone who loved him?

She sat on the bed, dry-eyed, staring blankly at the white stucco wall in front of her, the note still dangling from her limp hand. The minutes ticked by. She couldn't move. Her mind struggled to assimilate what had happened, but she had the odd feeling that she was standing outside herself, as a spectator, watching the woman on the bed from a distance, but not really involved.

What do I feel? she asked herself. Grief? No. That would come later. Right now I feel nothing, just this numb blankness, a state of shock similar to what the victim of a terrible accident experiences. She couldn't feel, couldn't think. She could only sit there.

Finally, after what seemed like hours, she crawled under the covers and closed her eyes, allowing herself to let go, to feel what was in her heart. Then the tears came, racking her body, tearing at her throat, soaking the pillow.

'But I *love* him!' she wailed aloud, over and over again.

It was the cruelty of it, she kept thinking. She had been willing to be patient, to do things his way. She hadn't pushed, hadn't asked for any commitment, any promises. Why couldn't he at least have stayed to say goodbye, to talk to her, explain his plans? Didn't he owe her that much? Was it really necessary to hurt her like this?

She slept at last, exhausted from the avalanche of emotion that had swept over her. She felt as though she was drowning, dying, and she didn't even care. She wanted to die. Jason Strong had revealed to her her capacity to love, then had taken it away. She knew she would never be the same.

When she woke up, the light was still burning in the bedroom. She felt disorientated, confused, and even reached for Jason, needing the reassurance of his presence beside her in the bed. When she realised he wasn't there, she remembered, and the awful pain of loss gripped her again.

This time, however, she didn't cry. She dimly realised that at some point in her agony the night before, she had touched bottom. Now all that remained was to climb slowly and steadily out of the pit she had allowed herself to fall into.

She sat up in bed, blinking. What time was it? She didn't know if it was morning or still the middle of the night. She got out of bed and went to the window. Methodically, she removed the bedspread she had placed in front of it that first night for Jason's protection.

Outside, the sun was just dawning. A rooster crowed from somewhere in the sleepy village. A dog barked. She stood at the window staring blankly out at the empty square, and once again she had the sensation that she was watching herself, testing herself to determine her true feelings.

What she felt, she realised with some surprise, was anger. The grief was gone, and in its place, growing with each passing moment, was a cold fury, a sense of such outrage at what Jason had done to her that she felt almost murderous. With it came a spark of the old determination that had seen her through all those long gruelling years of medical training, brought her to San Crístobal in the first place and kept her there, even in the face of danger.

With a renewed sense of purpose, she lifted her chin, set her shoulders, and turned from the window. She knew what she had to do now. She had been a fool, a blind, stupid, trusting fool, had fallen into the arms of the first man with an air of mystery about him who came along. Perhaps she had even needed the experience, she told herself as she made the bed. Like a painful vaccination against disease, now she would be immune against ever falling into that trap again.

She picked up the note he had left, tore it deliberately into tiny pieces and flushed it down the drain in the bathroom. There was no other trace of him in the house. As far as she was concerned, he didn't exist. She could wipe him out of her mind and heart until nothing of him remained to remind her of him.

Jessica spent the rest of that awful day in a nightmare of frenzied activity. Appalled at first at how much she had to do to be ready when Marshall came for her the next day, she soon saw that it was better to take one thing at a time and keep going than to stand and wring her hands over it.

She made her rounds in the village first. Luckily there were no emergency cases that needed her attention immediately, so at least she wouldn't feel guilty about leaving these simple people she had come to love. Once their trust had been gained, they had accepted her unreservedly, placing her second only to the village priest in their reverent affection.

At first she had thought she wouldn't tell them she was leaving. She just didn't think she could face their disappointment at the thought of losing their only doctor within miles. Finally, though, she knew she would have to face up to it, and it turned out to be even worse than she had feared.

Mrs Morales cried bitterly when Jessica told her. She tried to explain to her that her year was almost up anyway and a new doctor would be arriving shortly to take her place, but nothing she said seemed to make a difference. She left the Morales' hut at last, dejected and profoundly moved.

In the afternoon, she packed. She had only brought the minimum of supplies and medical equipment down with her. Most of the instruments and supplies in the surgery had been provided by the previous government and had been there when she arrived. All her personal medical paraphernalia fitted easily into her black bag. With luck, there would be a replacement for her sent to the village soon. Surely, she thought as she fitted the last of it into the bag, the agency that had sent her would have another doctor waiting.

By evening, she was worn out, but still in a curious state of heightened excitement at the same time. Just one day had brought about so many abrupt changes in her life—getting ready to leave, Jason's disappearance, saying goodbye to the villagers—that it was difficult to cope with calmly.

She went all over the house carefully, looking for any stray personal possessions she might have overlooked. At the same time, she knew she was also looking for some sign of Jason, some little thing he might have left behind that she could take with her to remember him by. She knew she was being perverse, but she couldn't help herself.

Of course, there was nothing. She had known there wouldn't be. He had come with so little, just the clothes on his back, a wallet with some money, identification and personal papers in it, that there was really nothing to leave. He hadn't even had pencil and paper to write on. Now that he was gone, the full force of his lack of personal belongings struck her, and she wondered how anyone could travel so lightly that he didn't even possess the tools of his trade.

She fixed herself a light supper of canned beans and fruit. Afterwards, as she washed up the few dishes she had used and put them away carefully in the cupboard, she couldn't help recalling all the pleasant evenings she and Jason had spent doing those homely little chores together, and the tears came unbidden, stinging her eyes then coursing down her cheeks until at last she leaned over the sink racked with terrible sobs.

She still felt jumpy when she got ready for bed that night. Wrung out emotionally to begin with, she had found it a long day, and she still had tomorrow to face. She only hoped that Marshall was right about being able to get her safely on a plane out of the country. A sudden longing for the safety and quiet of her home in Virginia seized her, and she finally decided to do something she had never done before, purely as an emergency measure. Before she got into bed, she swallowed a sleeping pill.

As the drug took effect and she began to grow drowsy, she found her dazed mind turning again to thoughts of Jason. It was bound to happen, she thought sadly. I can't expect to be rid of him, to get him out of my system, in one day. She reminded herself of his sudden departure, the brutal rejection. That was all there was worth remembering about him. The rest was like a dream, mere dust and ashes.

CHAPTER FIVE

'WELL, Jessie,' said her brother, 'how does it feel to be home?'

'It feels wonderful,' Jessica replied fervently.

She gave him a warm smile. He looked so solid and familiar sitting there on the couch, his long legs stretched out in front of him, his arms crossed behind his head. Tweedy was the word for Charles, she thought with affection. He was the typical college professor, with his muted herring-bone jacket, grey flannel trousers just a little baggy and silvery hair slightly rumpled.

'You still look too thin to me, though,' said Lisa.

Jessica sighed. Her brother's wife was a frustrated mother, and she thought once again what a pity it was they had never had children. All Lisa's maternal instinct had been turned on her ever since her parents died.

'I've only been home a month,' she said lightly to the older woman. 'Give me time.'

They were sitting in the living-room of her parents' old home in Taunton. A fire blazed in the hearth. It was early October, and already there was a hint of frost in the air.

'How's the job going?' Charles asked, straightening up and reaching for his pipe.

Jessica brightened. 'Quite well. It's just the kind of practice I hoped it would be. We get a little bit of everything, from broken bones to pregnancies.

Anything we can't handle, we send to a specialist in Washington.'

'Old Doc Weatherby's getting on, isn't he?' Charles asked, filling his pipe. 'He must be over seventy. I know he's been around for as long as I can remember.'

'He's still quite active, though, and I'm sure he intends to keep up his practice for a long time yet.'

Charles sucked on his pipe and gave her a shrewd look through the cloud of smoke that issued from it. 'Could work into a nice little partnership for you in time.'

Jessica shrugged. 'It's a little too soon to tell. I'm not making any plans too far in advance. I'm satisfied with what I'm doing right now.'

'Well,' said Lisa firmly, 'I only hope that means you're not going to go off to any more of those dangerous countries where there's a revolution every five minutes.'

'Don't worry, Lisa,' Jessica replied with feeling. 'I've had my fill of soldiers and shooting.'

'You must have been terrified out of your mind!' Lisa exclaimed.

'Not really,' Jessica said slowly. 'At the time I just did what I had to do and didn't think very much about it. I doubt if I was in any real danger.' She grinned mischievously. 'They needed me too much to kill me.'

Lisa made a face and shivered with distaste. 'Well, I'm just glad you're nice and safe back home where you belong.' She rose to her feet and held out a hand to her husband. 'Come on, old man. The Priors are coming to dinner tonight, and we've got to get back.'

'Tonight?' he exclaimed. 'It's Sunday!'

Lisa rolled her eyes then gave her husband a warm,

affectionate smile. 'Your brother thinks it's a law of nature that people don't entertain anyone except family on Sunday.' She turned to Jessica. 'Sure you won't join us, Jessica? The Priors would love to see you.'

Jessica shook her head firmly. 'No thanks. I've got early rounds at the hospital in the morning and should get to bed early.'

'Well, maybe next weekend then. There's a party at the Italian Embassy . . .'

'No, ma'am,' Charles announced, rising to his feet and knocking out his pipe in the ashtray. 'No more Embassy parties for me.'

'We'll see, darling,' said his wife placidly. 'We'll see.'

When they were gone, Jessica went back to the living-room and sat down in front of the fire to finish the Sunday paper, which was spread out over the coffee-table. She was glad Charles and Lisa had left early. They had driven out from Washington around noon with a supply of groceries and home-made cakes, just as though she wasn't capable of looking after herself. Jessica sighed as she turned the pages of the newspaper. She loved them both, and was grateful for their concern, but at twenty-eight, they really should stop treating her like a child.

She looked up from the paper after a few minutes and gazed idly around the familiar room. In one way, it still seemed odd to her to be back, but in another, it was as though she had never been away. Her year in San Crístobal seemed at times like a half-forgotten dream, but then, out of the blue, a sudden memory would rise up in her mind so vividly that she had to make an effort to shake it off and remind herself that it was only a part of the past.

She had lived in this house throughout all her childhood, first with her parents, then, after they were killed in the plane crash, with Charles and Lisa. After she went off to college, Charles had received his appointment at Georgetown University in Washington, and her brother and his wife had moved into a lovely modern apartment near the school.

Charles had wanted to sell the house then, but Jessica had begged him not to. Her roots were there. She needed to know it still belonged to her, even though she had agreed to rent it out for the year she would be in San Crístobal. Now the tenants were gone, as planned, and she had come straight home after the harrowing plane ride from Central America.

She had been lucky, too, she thought as she got up from the couch to put another log on the fire, that Dr Weatherby's offer to practise with him had still been open. She had started work at his family practice office just a week after she had arrived home, taking only the time she needed to get settled in the house again.

It was so good to be home, she thought as she walked over to the window. She pulled aside the curtain and looked outside at the long line of enormous old oak trees, flaming gold now, that rose up on both sides of the quiet residential street. Dr Weatherby's office was only five blocks away, and she hardly used the car in the garage except to drive into the city occasionally to shop or visit Charles and Lisa.

She turned and looked around the room with a deep sense of satisfaction and contentment. This was where she belonged, the blazing fire crackling on the hearth, her mother's good maple furniture placed where it had always been in the well-proportioned living room, the familiar Early American primitive paintings on the pale green walls, even the chipped Meissen plate on the coffee-table, filled with Lisa's home-made cakes.

It was a brilliant autumn day. Across the white picket fence she could see her nearest neighbour, old Mr Thorson, pruning his Paul's Scarlet climbing rose. A young boy rode by out in front on his bicycle, ringing his bell at a dog crossing the street lazily, and in the distance she could hear the low roar of a power mower. Soon it would be winter, it would snow, and she would be safe in her snug house.

Yes, she thought, as she dropped the curtain and went back to the couch. This is where I belong. No more revolutions for me. I need a nice, secure little world where I can do the work I love and live in peace.

The pot of tea she had made earlier was still warm, and she poured herself a cup now, sipping on it as she leafed through the newspaper. So many advertisements, she thought, and nothing but disasters all over the world.

Her eye was caught by a headline on the editorial page. 'Right-Wing Military Government Established in San Cristobal.' She was only mildly interested in the politics of that poor war-torn country, never having really understood what they were fighting about in the first place, but still, she thought, she should read the column just to see how the revolution had turned out.

Then she saw the by-line. Jason Strong. She slowly lowered her cup of tea back into its saucer, her hand trembling so that the two pieces of china clattered when they came together. Her heart began to thud painfully, and she had trouble focusing on the newspaper. The print seemed to be swimming before her eyes, and she read automatically, without understanding a word, just for something to do to steady her nerves.

Finally, she gave up. She leaned her head back on the couch and closed her eyes. This had been bound to happen eventually, she told herself. She had been quite successful in obliterating all thoughts of Jason Strong from her mind from the moment she had torn up that curt farewell note. At first, she had been too frantic to get packed and get out of the village to think about him. Then had come the bumpy jeep ride with Marshall over the unpaved mountain roads from the village to the capital. After that, it had been touch and go right up to the last minute whether she would even be able to get on a plane at all, and when she finally did, thanks to Marshall's bullying and, she suspected, outright bribery, it had flown an erratic, turbulent course that seemed to cover all Mexico and half the United States.

She had been so relieved to get home safely, then so busy getting the house in shape and starting her job, that the whole experience in San Cristobal had conveniently been forgotten. That's what she had thought, at any rate. Until today.

Now, the whole thing came flooding back into her mind, and the pain of it was so intense that she could scarcely breathe. After several moments, she got to her feet and started pacing about the living-room. Why, she asked herself, does the memory of him still have such power to hurt me? She searched her mind for an answer.

Surely it wasn't her blighted love, or missing him, or wanting him back that caused the searing pain in her heart and mind? No, she decided, as she paced; it wasn't any of those things. It couldn't be, not after he walked out on me so callously. What was tearing her apart, what she wanted so desperately to forget, was the awful humiliation of it.

She sat back down heavily on the couch and reached for her cup. The tea was cold by now, but she drank it anyway, not really tasting it, and stared into the flickering flames. A surge of self-loathing swept over her. She had given herself unreservedly to this man, she thought bitterly, just like a silly teenager with her first crush. She shuddered with the self-contempt that filled her. She longed to lash out, to hit something, and had to resist the impulse to throw her mother's treasured Meissen cup up against the fireplace.

I can't even blame him, she thought sadly when she was calmer. I should have known what kind of man he was. He never lied to me, never made any promises. The lovely future I had planned was all in my own mind; he probably has had similar encounters all over the world. It was no big deal to him, and it wasn't his fault that it was my first experience with such a consuming passion.

She felt so cheapened, she thought disgustedly. What I imagined was a transcendent love turned out to be only a crippling physical desire, only sex, pure and simple. And if I feel used, betrayed, it's my own fault.

Jessica got up and walked to the window again. The sky was gradually becoming overcast, a sudden brisk wind pulling a bank of heavy rain clouds across the darkening sky.

'I made a stupid mistake,' she said aloud to the empty room. But, just below the surface of her reasoned objectivity, a banked fire of resentment smouldered against the man who had hurt her so badly. Regardless of whose fault it was, she could not forget that, mistaken as she might have been, at the time she had been convinced that he did care for her in his own way. What it boiled down to, then, was that he had deceived her about his feelings just to get her into bed.

She clenched her fists at her sides as another spasm of rage and humiliation flooded over her. But it will never happen again, she vowed silently.

As the days passed and she settled into a busy routine, Jessica found that the painful memories did begin to fade once more. She still felt a sharp stab of shame and resentment whenever she thought about it, but she knew it would be a mistake to let it fester, and each time it hurt just a little less. In time, she hoped, the whole shabby episode would be forgotten.

Two weeks later, on another crisp October afternoon, she was out in the front yard raking up the leaves that were dropping fast from the maple trees when she heard the telephone ringing inside the house. She stood there, rake in hand, debating for a moment whether to answer it. She had wanted to get done before the sun went down so that she could add her pile to Mr Thorson's bonfire, which was burning next door.

She knew she had to answer it, however; she was on call that weekend, and it could be an emergency. She laid her rake down and ran into the house through the back door. A little out of breath, she picked up the telephone on the kitchen counter.

'Hello.'

'Jessica, it's Marshall. Marshall Bennett.'

'Marshall?' She sat down on the nearby stool. 'Where in the world are you? The last time I saw you, you had just shoved me on to that awful airplane, and I was waving goodbye to you.'

He laughed. 'That was quite a dramatic escape. Well engineered, too, if I do say so myself,' he added smugly.

'Well engineered!' she snorted. 'That's a laugh! How much did you have to pay that soldier at the last minute?'

'We don't need to go into that,' he said firmly. 'I got you out, didn't I?'

'Yes, Marshall, you got me out, and I'm grateful. Now, where are you calling from? Zaire? Afghanistan? Iraq?'

'Washington,' he said.

'Washington? You mean, Washington, D.C.?'

'That's right. After we got kicked out of San Cristobal by the new military government, the State Department brought me back here for reassignment.'

'And what lovely place will they send you to next?'

'Who knows? I may stay here permanently. At least, that's what I've put in for. I'm getting a little too old for these trouble spots.'

'Sure, Marshall,' she said drily. 'You must be all of thirty-five.'

'Thirty-three, actually, but I'm very mature for my age. I'm not kidding, Jessica, I've really had it with wild-eyed revolutionaries and trigger-happy insurgents. It's time for me to settle down, start thinking about a permanent home, a family.'

'Why, Marshall, I'm surprised at you,' she teased. 'Here I've thought of you all along as a swashbuckling soldier of fortune.'

'Sorry to disappoint you, Jessica,' he said cheerfully. 'But it's pipe-and-slippers time for me. I might even get a dog.'

Actually, Jessica thought, smiling, the pipe-and-slippers image fitted Marshall far better than that of soldier of fortune. He was a large, rather placid man, whose exploits on her behalf down in San Cristobal had seemed out of character.

'Well, I'm inclined to agree with you,' she said. 'I'm more than ready to bid a fond farewell to life in the fast lane.'

'I'm very glad to hear that, Jessica,' he said in a low, more sober tone. He hesitated a moment, then cleared his throat. 'Which brings me to the reason for my call. How would you like to put on your most glamorous party dress and attend a ball with me?'

'A ball? My goodness, Marshall, I haven't been dancing since . . . Well, it seems like for ever. I don't even own a party dress!'

'You do know how to dance?'

'Well, yes, of course I do, but . . .'

'There are dress shops out there in the wilds of Taunton?' he went on.

'Yes,' she said, laughing.

'Well, then? What's the problem?' Then, on a more serious note, he said, 'Come on, Jessica. I'd really like to have you come.'

'When is this great ball, Marshall? And where?'

'Saturday night at the French Embassy. The food will be superb, and the vintage champagne will flow like water. I'll even come all the way out to Taunton and pick you up. What do you say?'

'*All* the way out here?' she mimicked drily. 'Your generosity overwhelms me. What is it, a gruelling half-hour drive from Washington on the freeway?'

'Well . . .'

'Never mind, Marshall. I'll drive in myself.' And drive home alone, she added to herself.

They arranged to meet at the Embassy on Saturday night at eight o'clock and hung up.

She had mixed feelings about going out with Marshall. She liked him, she thought, as she went back outside to finish her raking, and it would be fun to go to a real ball again. It had been years since she'd got all dressed up to go to an elegant social affair, not since her college days, and she knew a lot of people in Washington she would like very much to see again.

On the other hand, she didn't like the noises Marshall was making about settling down, raising a family. If he has me in mind as a likely candidate, she thought as she drew on her gloves and picked up the rake where she had dropped it, the situation could get sticky.

The firm conviction that she wanted no part of a romantic involvement with Marshall surprised her a little, both in its suddenness and its intensity. There was simply, all at once, no question in her mind about it. It was as though her experience with Jason Strong had left her missing a part of herself, even emotionally crippled. The thought of ever giving herself to another man, of allowing even the slightest move towards a relationship of that kind, simply left her cold.

It was out of the question, she vowed, attacking the remaining scattered leaves viciously. Not only did she feel that she could never trust her judgment about men again after the searing humiliation inflicted on her by Jason, but, at bottom, she didn't even want to fall in love. She had her work, her home. That would be enough.

                         *   *   *

The next day Jessica went about her daily rounds as usual. She was beginning to feel comfortable in the routine Dr Weatherby had established in his office, and now that she was better acquainted with his procedures and the patients he had turned over to her, she enjoyed the work far more than she thought she would after the excitement of San Crístobal.

It came as a pleasant surprise to her, too, to find that not only was she not mistrusted or avoided just because she was a woman, as she had feared, but many patients considered it a positive asset.

'I can talk to you,' confided old Mrs Columbo, as Jessica gently examined her arthritic hands. 'I just feel more comfortable with a woman doctor.'

It wasn't only the women patients who felt that way, either. Children were not nearly so frightened of her as they were the sterner, more remote Dr Weatherby, and there were even a few men who had begun to call for appointments with 'the lady doctor.'

She had had a little trouble at first with Mrs Schultz, the doctor's nurse of many years. The older woman was naturally a little wary of her, Jessica realised right from the beginning, not only because she had never worked with a woman doctor before, but also because she was afraid Jessica might usurp her function as Dr Weatherby's trusted right hand.

However, once Jessica recognised Mrs Schultz's fears, she went out of her way to demonstrate to her that as doctor and nurse, their duties would not overlap. As far as her efficacy as a medical practitioner went, only time could prove to the rather stern, grey-haired nurse that Jessica really was qualified and really did know what she was doing.

Even though Jessica had chosen a career largely dominated by men, she had done so out of a genuine sense of vocation, and not to prove anything to the world about the ability of a woman to do whatever a man could do. She became a doctor because she wanted to practise medicine, period. Thus, she understood and accepted the realities of her situation, well aware that she would have to overcome some prejudice against it. She had decided early that the best way to do this was not to adopt a strident, aggressive attitude and demand universal recognition of her 'rights' immediately, but simply to put her energies into being the best doctor she could be.

At noon, she had finished with her last morning appointment and was sitting in her small office at the back of the building, directly across the corridor from Dr Weatherby's larger one. Down the hall were four examination rooms, two on each side, a lavatory, a small lab; then, in front, the waiting-room and Mrs Schultz's domain behind a waist-high counter, where all the files were kept and appointments made.

Today, Monday, was Dr Weatherby's day off, and Jessica wondered if she would have time to do a little shopping before her first afternoon appointment at half-past one. If she hurried, she thought, and went without lunch, and there were no emergencies, she should be able to make it.

After she had finished her raking yesterday and gone inside to make dinner, it had dawned on her that she really had absolutely nothing to wear to the ball on Saturday night. She had been too poor to afford many clothes while she was interning, and in her year in San Cristobal she hadn't needed them.

Making up her mind to chance a short shopping expedition, she put on the jacket to her oatmeal-tweed woollen suit, found her large leather handbag, and went out the back door of the office to the street at the back.

Taunton was quite a small town, with a business district only five or six blocks long. As she walked down Main Street, peering into shop windows, she wondered if the town even boasted a dress shop, much less one that would carry any selection at all in ball gowns. Washington was so close that the residents had formed the habit of doing all their serious shopping in the city.

She did remember one rather nice shop where Lisa had found some good things when she and Charles had lived in Taunton. It was expensive, Jessica recalled, as she headed across the street towards the place where it used to stand, run by two elderly sisters who had 'come down in the world', but who had a remarkable clothes sense. It was even doubtful if it was still there.

But it was, and just the same as she remembered it. There was just the one discreet sign in the window, silver letters on a black enamel background—Cabots—Ladies' Apparel—and what appeared to be the same two old-fashioned mannequins in the same stilted posture, one blonde, one brunette. The brunette was wearing a well cut, conservative woollen suit in a soft reddish shade, and the blonde a perfectly plain but absolutely stunning long dress of champagne-coloured silk. It looked like peau-de-soie to Jessica, quite light-weight, but somewhat stiff, and she stood for several moments gazing at it covetously.

Finally she went inside. A little bell tinkled at the top of the door, and in a moment a white-haired woman, thin and erect, came out from the back of the shop. It was one of the Miss Cabots.

'May I help you?' she asked politely.

'The silk dress in the window,' said Jessica. 'Would

you have it in my size?'

'I'll have to see,' replied Miss Cabot primly. 'All our garments are one-of-a-kind. That one is a size eight.' She gave Jessica a practised appraising sweep of her eyes, then nodded. 'Yes, I think it might do. Why don't you go into the dressing-room in the back while I take it off the mannequin.'

After she had undressed and Miss Cabot had returned to help her on with the gown, Jessica gazed into the full-length mirror, hoping the dress looked as good on her as it felt.

It was perfect, she thought, as she examined her reflection. The wide, low-scooped neck just skimmed the tops of her breasts, which filled the bodice to perfection.

'Yes, indeed,' came Miss Cabot's voice from beside her. 'Ladylike, but slightly suggestive. The colour is perfect for you with your nice honey-blonde hair.' She tugged gently at the waistline. 'A little loose here, but a tiny alteration will fix that.'

'I'll take it,' Jessica said at last.

When she heard the price she almost fainted, but then, she thought, I can afford it now, and it's a dress I can wear over and over again. It was cut so perfectly and in such a subtle style and colour, that people would notice her in it rather than the dress itself.

On Saturday night Jessica dressed carefully. It had been so long since she had paid close attention to her appearance that she had a little trouble even getting started. In the past few years she had been too busy to cultivate the art of make-up or to experiment with hairstyles, outside of a dash of lipstick and keeping her hair clean and well brushed.

Tonight, however, she wanted to do justice to the

beautiful new dress. At six o'clock, she sat in front of
her dressing-table in her robe, a towel wrapped
around her freshly washed hair, staring down at the
array of cosmetics she had purchased that day. The
girl in the shop had advised her what she would need
and told her the order in which to apply the contents
of each mysterious container, but she had been
practising for an hour and still couldn't use them
properly.

There was foundation cream, blusher, liquid
make-up, loose powder, eye-liner, mascara, eye-
shadow, eyebrow pencil and a few odd little boxes
she couldn't even remember buying. She looked
askance at the tiny jar of lip-gloss and the sable brush
that had come with it. She had very steady hands, but
when she had practised using the brush to outline the
contours of her mouth, she had ended up with a
smeared mess that in no way conformed to them.

The eye make-up was a similar disaster. Her
eyelashes were so long that she had dripped mascara
on her cheeks and eyelids just by blinking a few
times, and the shadow and liner made her look like a
raccoon. The blusher never seemed to *blend* properly,
as the girl had told her it should, and each time she
had tried to use it, she had just sat and stared at the
two bright red spots on her cheeks—in the wrong
place, naturally.

It will come with practice, the salesgirl had
promised, and Jessica believed her. The trouble was,
she didn't have time. Not only that, but she wasn't at
all sure she wanted to learn. She glanced ruefully at
her reflection in the mirror and made a face at the
painted image that gazed back at her. It was a
profoundly depressing sight.

She glanced at her watch. It was six-thirty already.

She'd have to leave in an hour, and she hadn't even dried her hair. Panic began to rise up in her. There just wasn't time to perfect her make-up technique tonight, and that's all there was to it. The dress would have to speak for itself without any help from her.

Once she made up her mind, she felt much better, even a little silly for having worried about it. After all, she muttered to herself as she scrubbed off the botched-up *maquillage*, I've lived twenty-eight years in total ignorance of the art of making myself beautiful. One more night won't make any difference.

She ended by using only the foundation lotion, a light dusting of powder, her trusty old tube of pale lipstick and one gentle swipe of mascara for each eye. She blew her hair dry, brushed the long golden strands until they gleamed, then pinned it loosely up on top of her head. There was enough natural curl to give it the body it needed, but at the last minute she gave it one sweeping shot of hair spray.

'Not bad,' she told her reflection when she had finished. Not exactly glamorous, she added silently, but definitely presentable.

She took off her robe and slipped into the dress. Miss Cabot had taken in the waistline so that it fitted her to perfection now. The low neckline was not actually revealing, but did hint at the fullness beneath it. The stiff material was sewn into tiny unpressed pleats at the waist and flared into a long skirt just full enough to appear festive without making her look like Marie Antoinette.

No jewellery, she decided, at least not at her neck. She didn't want anything to detract from the dress. She got out her mother's pearl teardrop earrings and fastened them, then stood back and surveyed the overall effect.

The glamour girls of Washington society were in no danger, she finally decided, but for a small-town doctor, I'll at least pass. The dress was wonderful, her hair shone, the earrings gleamed, and if her make-up job left something to be desired, she still felt she had achieved a happy medium between a bare, naked look and over-painting.

She collected her handbag and gloves, put on her good black woollen coat, and went out to the garage, locking the house up tight behind her. She had already practised driving Charles's old Thunderbird. It was his pride and joy, but of no use to him in the city, and he had given her permission to use it.

As she drove towards the city in the early autumn darkness, she had to admit that she was looking forward to the ball with pleasurable anticipation. She even managed to laugh at herself for her earlier worries over her appearance.

After all, she thought, as she exited off the freeway on to the beltway that ringed the city, it's only Marshall.

He was waiting for her when she pulled up in front of the French Embassy, standing on the steps near the brightly lit entrance and looking tall and solid and handsome in his white tie and black tails.

When he saw her, he raised a hand in greeting and came down to the kerb to speak to her through the car window.

'Just leave it here,' he said. 'One of the attendants will be along soon and park it for you.'

Jessica glanced around. There were several people milling about—couples in formal attire—and it seemed safe enough. She got out of the car and came to stand beside Marshall on the pavement.

'I hope you're right,' she said. 'Charles will murder me if anything happens to his precious Thunderbird. I feel as though I've been entrusted with the Crown jewels.'

Marshall eyed the powerful car covetously. 'A valuable antique, at any rate. That model is worth a fortune these days.' Then he turned to her, bowed stiffly and crooked his arm. 'Shall we make our grand entrance?'

She dipped a mock curtsy and took his arm. 'Let's.'

They started up the wide front steps. The entrance doors were wide open and Jessica could hear orchestra music drifting outside through them. Several other couples were moving up the stairs along with them, greeting each other in loud voices, their conversations punctuated with bursts of laughter.

As they walked, Marshall tucked her arm firmly under his and gazed down at her. 'I'm so glad you came, Jessica. You look very lovely.' He laughed. 'Quite a transformation from the last time I saw you.'

He gave the attendant at the entrance his invitation card, and they went inside. The music was much louder now, and the foyer quite crowded.

'I'll check your coat,' said Marshall, slipping it off her shoulders. 'Then we can go inside and find our table.'

She waited for him beside a wide curving staircase, clutching her handbag and staring, fascinated by the crowds of people surging past her. The women were dressed in every conceivable style, from the most elegant long brocaded ball-gowns to the shortest, slinkiest miniskirt. As she surveyed the motley array, she felt more and more confident of her own choice of dress. The silk gown was exactly right, just festive enough without appearing ostentatious.

The men were all dressed pretty much alike, she saw, at least as to colour. They all wore formal dark dress suits, and she envied them the simplicity of their grooming. No struggles with make-up or hair styles or fashion, just find a good tailor for fit and that's all there was to it. Funny, she mused, as she watched them, people never spoke of 'dowdy' men or 'cheap' men. Fat, thin, short, tall, dark or fair, in a sense they all looked alike, protected by their uniformity of dress. That very conformity seemed to provide them a sort of freedom just to be who they were, without labels.

As she mulled over this paradox, her glance fell on a striking-looking couple just coming in through the entrance. As though to prove her point, her eye was caught first by the woman, a tall redhead wearing a bright emerald-green dress, cut extremely low, her neck, ears and wrists blazing with diamonds.

Well, she thought idly, if you dress to attract attention, that's what you'll get. She shifted her gaze to the man behind the redhead, and drew in her breath sharply as she instantly recognised Jason Strong. There was no mistaking that proud carriage, the gaunt dark face, the secretive hooded eyes.

The shock of seeing him again when she least expected it hit her like a physical blow. She closed her eyes and swayed weakly, her blood running first hot, then cold, her heart thudding so erratically that it pounded wildly in her ears. She clutched a hand at her throat and groped blindly with the other one for some support. The one thing she was terrified of was fainting, and she summoned up all her power of will to get herself under control before Marshall returned.

Her hand finally came to rest on the newel-post of

the banister behind her, and she turned around sharply, leaning against the railing. Gradually, her breathing returned to normal. She turned slowly back towards the entrance again and glanced sideways in that direction.

He was gone, probably carried along into the adjacent ballroom on the tide of people moving toward it. He mustn't see me, she thought fiercely. I couldn't bear that.

CHAPTER SIX

'ARE you all right, Jessica?'

Marshall was standing beside her now, a worried look on his broad, bland face. She nodded and forced out a smile.

'Yes. Of course. Just a little overwhelmed by the crowd. I'm not used to civilisation yet, I guess. Maybe if you could find the powder-room for me, I'll take a short breather before we make our grand entrance.'

She gave him a reassuring look, and after a moment's hesitation, he grinned back at her and took her by the arm.

'*That*, at least, I can help you with. I know these embassies like the back of my hand. Just follow me.'

The powder-room was on the main floor. It was decorated in a predictably elegant, very French style, with grey and white striped wallpaper, graceful little white chairs in front of a long tiled counter, and lavish bright pink touches in the thick carpet and velveteen cushions.

Several women were inside, standing around in groups, smoking, chatting or repairing their make-up and coiffures at the wide mirror above the counter. As Jessica walked past them, she could feel their speculative eyes on her, carefully assessing her appearance, as though judging the competition.

Inside the grey and pink tiled lavatory, she ran cool water over her wrists and tried to pull her scattered thoughts together. It was the sudden, unexpected sight of him, she thought, that had hit her so hard. Somehow, she had had it firmly fixed in her mind that she would never see him again, and she realised that this thought had given her a measure of protection from painful emotion, even made her feel safe.

Now, however, it all came rushing back—the love, the passion, the total absorption in another human being. And, she added, the humiliation, the rage. In a sense, Jason Strong had been dead to her, and the sight of him tonight was like the sudden appearance of a spectre from the grave.

She stared at her reflection in the mirror and wondered how she had managed to convince herself she would never see him again. He had told her his home base was in Washington. Given his prominence in the field of political journalism, he would naturally move freely within the city's tight social circles.

It was time to get back. The one thing she wanted to avoid was alerting Marshall to any connection with this man. No one knew they had ever even met before. Chances were they would never meet again. The painful memory had faded once, she told herself, and it would do so again.

Marshall was standing by the door to the powder-room patiently waiting for her when she emerged. The sight of his large, comforting presence gave her that last little bit of courage she needed, and she gave him a grateful smile as she took his arm.

'Feeling better?' he asked.

'Fine. No problem.'

'I have a surprise for you,' he said as he led her into the ballroom. 'A pleasant one, I hope.'

They threaded their way around the edge of the

large dance floor towards the cluster of tables surrounding it. The floor was brightly lit and filled with dancing couples. The music was much louder in here, but quite danceable, with a steady, bouncy beat. The fringe area, where the small tables were set out, was very dim, lit only by the flickering candles in the centre of each one.

She wondered what Marshall meant by his surprise. It was too noisy for her to be heard to ask him now, and she only hoped it wouldn't be as unsettling a jolt as the one she had just experienced.

Marshall greeted several people on the way to their table, introducing Jessica whenever he stopped. He had been in government service for ten years or more by now, and had made many acquaintances on his various tours of duty. The diplomatic corps was like a small, tightly knit fraternity, where the same people would crop up in different places all over the world.

When Marshall stopped finally at a table for four, with two people already seated, Jessica could only stare. Sitting there, looking glum and uncomfortable in his worn tuxedo, was her brother, Charles, with a smug, complacent Lisa beside him.

'Surprise!' Lisa called, waving them forward.

Jessica stood over her brother, staring down at him. 'Charles! I don't believe it! Just a few weeks ago I heard you claim you'd never go to another embassy party.'

Charles untangled his long legs and rose slowly to his feet. 'I have Lisa to thank for my broken vow,' he said with a jerk of his head towards his beaming wife. 'In case you hadn't noticed, that frail-looking exterior of hers masks a will of iron.'

Jessica glanced down at her sister-in-law with an amused smile. Lisa grinned back at her broadly and waved them to the vacant chairs.

'Sit down, sit down,' she called over the din of the music. 'Don't pay any attention to him,' she muttered in a low voice when Jessica was seated next to her. 'He loves it, but just doesn't like to admit it.'

'You're sure about that?' said Jessica with mock solemnity.

'Oh, yes. You wait and see. Two glasses of champagne and a plate of coq au vin and he'll even dance with me.'

Charles only grunted and began to fill his pipe. Marshall had remained standing, and he leaned over the table to speak to Jessica.

'What'll it be, Jessica? Champagne or a dance?'

'Oh, champagne, please. I haven't danced for so long that I need a little fortification before I venture out on to the dance floor.'

Marshall hailed a passing waiter, plucked two glasses off his tray, and sat down beside Jessica. 'Here,' he said, handing her a glass. 'This should be the real stuff. I think they bring it in by diplomatic courier by the case. No duty to pay.'

Jessica raised her glass to his and touched it lightly.

'Cheers,' she said, and took a long swallow of the cold, bubbly wine. 'I'm no connoisseur, but it tastes wonderful to me.'

As the evening progressed, Jessica began to relax and enjoy herself. Occasionally, as she danced with Marshall or Charles, she would imagine that she spotted the familiar dark head across the sea of people on the dance floor, but it was so crowded and noisy that she could never be sure.

At precisely midnight, Charles knocked out the smouldering remains of his pipe into the ashtray on the table, abruptly rose to his feet, and stood looking down at his wife with a look of firm determination on his long, normally mild face.

'Time to go home, Lisa,' he announced with no preamble.

Lisa, deeply involved in a conversation with Marshall over the latest marital scandal involving a high-ranking member of Congress, gazed up at her husband with melting brown eyes.

'Yes, dear. Of course.'

Jessica, who had been contentedly gazing out at the dancing crowd, sipping her third glass of champagne and listening to the music, stared at Lisa in surprise. She had never known her to be so docile. Then, with an amused smile at Marshall, who had been left with a half-finished sentence on his lips when Charles interrupted, she settled back in her chair to watch what promised to be an interesting insight into the workings of her brother's marriage.

Lisa immediately gathered her gloves and handbag together and got up from her chair. She gave Jessica one brief conspiratorial glance, then put her arm through her husband's and smiled sweetly at him. He looked a little startled at Lisa's sudden docility, but then a slow, self-satisfied grin began to spread over his face and he nodded cheerfully at Jessica and Marshall.

'Well, good night, you two. It's been a pleasant evening, but it's time to get these old bones to bed.'

'Oh, don't say good night yet, darling,' Lisa purred. 'Jessica, you and Marshall will stop by, won't you? A few people are dropping in at our place for a nightcap. In fact, why not plan to spend the night? There's no need for you to drive back to Taunton at this hour. Marshall can bring you to our place, and you can pick up your car tomorrow.'

When Jessica saw Charles's stricken expression at the prospect of a continuation of the party, and at his own house, to boot, she could barely stifle a giggle. He turned to Lisa with murder in his eyes, his mouth open, ready to do battle, but before he could say a word, she stood up on tiptoe and planted a kiss on his cheek.

'I'm so glad you want to leave early, darling. I told everyone to be there at twelve-thirty, and now we can get to bed at a decent hour. Just a few people, and they won't stay long. Come on, now, we'd better hurry.'

With one last triumphant grin at Jessica, she began to pull Charles away from the table. He gave Marshall a grim look, then shrugged helplessly and turned to follow his wife.

The minute they were out of earshot, Marshall and Jessica took one look at each other, then burst out laughing.

'That sister-in-law of yours has missed her calling,' Marshall said at last when he could speak. 'She'd be the director of the diplomatic corps by now. Even Secretary of State.'

'She's a master at handling Charles, at any rate,' Jessica agreed.

Marshall shook his head. 'That was one of the neatest jobs of manipulation I've ever seen.' He started to laugh again. 'Poor Charles never knew what hit him.'

'You'd think after all these years he'd have caught on to her game,' Jessica smiled. 'He must like it.'

'How long have they been married?'

'Let's see, our parents died when I was ten. That's eighteen years ago, and they were newly-weds then. It must be almost twenty years.'

'And he's still like putty in her hands.'

'Well,' said Jessica with a shrug, 'he loves her. And he knows she loves him, in spite of her manoeuvring. That's the really important aspect of their relationship.'

Marshall leaned towards her, his gaze softening as their eyes met. He reached for her hand. The gesture made her a little uneasy. She hadn't forgotten what he had said on the telephone about wanting to settle down.

'That's what matters most, isn't it, Jessica?' he asked in a low intimate tone. 'Loving each other, building a life, a home, a future together.'

'Yes, of course,' said Jessica hesitantly. 'I suppose it does. It depends on the people, of course. They both have to want the same thing.'

'What do you want, Jessica?' he asked.

His hand tightened on hers. She noted nervously that the look in his eyes had become downright soulful. I've got to put a stop to this right now, she thought wildly. She gently withdrew her hand and pushed her chair back.

'Right now, I think I'd like one last dance. Do you feel up to it?'

She winced inwardly at the hurt look in his eyes, but she stood her ground. Better to bruise his ego a little now, she thought, than to allow him to plan on a future that couldn't possibly work out and end up by really hurting him.

He held her a little stiffly as they danced, and although she did feel sorry for him, she was determined not to let him force her into a relationship that didn't attract her in the least. She liked him, she hoped they could remain friends, but he would have to understand right now that an emotional attachment of any kind was out of the question.

She began asking him about his work, always a fascinating topic of conversation for most men, she had noticed, and by the end of the dance he had thawed considerably. When the music died away, they threaded their way off the dance floor and back to their table.

'It's almost twelve-thirty,' he said. 'If we're going on to Lisa's get-together, we probably should leave now.'

She gave him a dubious look. 'I don't know, Marshall,' she said slowly. 'Do you really want to go? It's already quite late.'

'Do you have to work tomorrow?'

'No. This is my weekend off. Dr Weatherby's on call.'

He shrugged his shoulders. 'Well, let's go, then. Lisa's parties are always interesting. She knows everyone in Washington.'

'As well as Virginia, Maryland and Pennsylvania,' Jessica added with a smile.

Her brother's apartment was in the Georgetown section of Washington, not far from the Embassy, and it only took them fifteen minutes to get there. It was a quiet, tree-lined street of old brick houses interspersed with modern apartment buildings, all of them beautifully kept in this pleasantest of the city's districts.

Marshall found a parking space just a few doors down, not so difficult at this hour of the morning. He pulled into it, shut off the engine and turned to Jessica. She sat stiffly beside him, waiting, an unpleasant premonition already forming in her mind that a sticky scene was about to take place.

'Jessica,' he said. 'There's something I'd like to discuss before we go inside.'

She turned to him. 'Marshall . . .' she began.

He held up a hand. 'Please. Just let me have my say.'

There was a full moon in the dark night sky overhead, shining directly in through the front windscreen, casting a silvery glow on the deserted street. From the distance came the wail of a siren. It grew louder, then faded away into silence. Jessica waited, her hands folded in her lap.

Finally he spoke. 'Do you remember what I said the other day on the telephone? About thinking it's time I settled down?'

She glanced at him. His face was solemn in the moonlight. He looked big and solid and kind, and although she found his insistence exasperating after she had tried to warn him off earlier, she began to have second thoughts. If she ever intended to marry, make a home, have a family, she couldn't possibly ask for a better candidate than Marshall to share that kind of life.

'Yes,' she said slowly. 'I remember.'

'We've known each other for quite a while,' he went on. 'In fact,' he said with a grin, 'we've been through some pretty harrowing experiences together.' He frowned. 'What I'm trying to say is that I'd like us to get to know each other even better.' He put a hand tentatively on her shoulder. 'I like you a lot, Jessica,' he said in a voice husky with emotion. 'In fact, I might even be half in love with you. What do you think? Is there a chance you might come to feel that way about me?'

She waited a long time to answer. Marshall was one of the finest men she had ever met. Not only did she not want to hurt him, but it would be foolish to reject him prematurely, just because he didn't set her pulses racing or her blood singing—only one man had done that, and she had lived to regret it bitterly.

'I don't know, Marshall,' she said at last. 'I don't think I'm ready for any kind of—well—serious relationship. This last year has been chaos for me. You know that. I'm just beginning to stabilise my life, get moving ahead in my work, establish some kind of permanency and security. To change it now ... Well, I just don't think I could face it.'

'I can understand that,' he said hastily. 'And I won't rush you.' He laughed drily. 'I guess what I'm really asking is whether you're so totally against the idea that I'd be wasting my time pursuing it at all. I mean, if you find me repulsive and I turn you off completely, what's the point?'

She didn't know what to say. She wanted to be fair to him. It would be wrong to encourage him, when she was virtually certain in her deepest self that the kind of relationship he seemed to want from her was not possible, but on the other hand, she did like him very much. He was reliable, thoughtful, and without a trace of the arrogance or cynicism she had seen in Jason Strong. With him, she would always felt shut out, as though he had deliberately put up invisible barriers she didn't dare cross, while Marshall was open and above board about everything.

'No, Marshall, of course you're not repulsive to me. It's not you at all.' She shook her head sadly. 'I don't ... I'm pretty well convinced that the kind of ... ship you're talking about just isn't on the ... me.'

' ... right now? Or ever?'

'Probably ever.' She smiled wanly. 'Maybe I'm just cold.'

'I can't believe that!' he said warmly. 'I saw the way you cared for those villagers in San Crístobal. Your feeling for them was genuine. There's a lot of love in you, Jessica; I can sense it.'

'But that's just the point, don't you see? Perhaps the reason I can love people who need me, my skills as a doctor, is the same reason I can't love an individual.' Not after Jason, she added to herself. He cured me of that kind of foolishness for good. She reached for the door handle. 'Come on. If we're going to Lisa's party, we'd better get moving.'

She knew he wasn't satisfied with her response, but it was all she could give him right now. He followed her reluctantly up the front steps of the apartment house, neither of them saying a word. She suddenly felt very tired. The agonising preparations for the ball, the hours of dancing, the conversation with Marshall, and seeing Jason again—especially that—had worked on her nerves so that she felt drained of energy.

Charles and Lisa occupied the entire ground floor of their building and had their own private entrance. The front door was slightly ajar, and through it Jessica could hear music and the sounds of laughter and conversation coming from inside.

'There's no point in knocking,' she said. 'They'd never hear us. We might as well just go on in.'

Marshall reached in front of her to push the door open, and they went inside. There was a small foyer with a black and white tiled floor. Coats were hung on an ancient clothes rack, as well as strewn over a small settee placed in front of an ornate gilt-framed mirror.

Jessica placed her coat on top of the pile, then gave herself a quick glance in the mirror. It was slightly damp outside, and a few tendrils of blonde hair had escaped the pins. As she was tucking them up, Lisa appeared in the archway that led into the sitting-room.

'There you are,' she called. 'Come inside. Everyone else is already here.' She put her arm through Jessica's and led her away with Marshall right behind them. 'What kept you so long?'

Jessica could feel herself reddening. 'Oh, we danced a little more, then we—er—talked for a while.'

Lisa's eyebrows flew up. 'Ah, I see,' she said in a low voice. 'That sounds interesting.'

Jessica turned to her, about to deliver a sharp retort, but before she had the chance, they were inside the long, high-ceilinged sitting-room. It was quite a large room, but still it seemed to be filled with people. She gave Lisa a wry glance.

'Just a few people?' she murmured.

But Lisa had darted off by then. Jessica glanced around the room. She recoqnised several old friends, some colleagues of Charles's from the university, and a few faces she had seen in the newspapers. She turned to Marshall.

'Shall we get a drink? I think we might need one.'

A harried-looking Charles was tending bar at the far end of the room near the fireplace, which crackled with burning logs. As they moved towards him through the crowd, Jessica spoke to a few people, some of whom she was genuinely glad to see after her long absence from home. Gradually she felt herself relax and even start to enjoy herself.

'Lisa has a talent for collecting just the right

combination of people at her parties,' she said to
Marshall as they approached the bar. 'I've never yet
known one to fail.'

Marshall smiled warmly down at her. 'As I said
before, she's a lady of many talents.'

Charles was busily mixing drinks and trying to
smoke his pipe at the same time. Jessica perched
herself on a high stool in front of the bar, leaned her
elbows on top of it and cupped her chin in her hands,
staring at him until he looked up from his chores.

'Hello, Charles,' she said with a grin. 'You look
like the proverbial one-armed paperhanger.'

He only grunted and set down his pipe. 'Well,' he
said, 'she did it again. Manoeuvred me not only into
attending another Embassy Ball when I swore I'd
never do it again, but into making drinks for another
houseful of people. That woman will be the death of
me!' He gave her a morose look. 'And you think it's
funny,' he accused glumly.

'Oh, Charles, don't be an old grouch.' She was
trying hard not to smile. 'In your heart you know you
love it.'

He raised his eyebrows at her. 'Oh, do I, now?
That's news to me. Now, what will you have to
drink?'

'Let's see,' she said, furrowing her brow. 'Something difficult and fancy, I think. How about a Pink
Lady? Or maybe a Brandy Alexander.'

'You get Scotch or bourbon, and that's it,' he said
flatly. 'Marshall, what'll it be?'

'Well, hell, Charles, I was hoping for a Grasshop-
per, but if your talents only reach as far as simple
highballs, make mine Scotch.'

Even Charles had to smile at that, and as he mixed
their drinks, Jessica swivelled on her stool to face

Marshall, who was standing close beside her, grinning down at her.

'It seems a shame,' she said with mock resignation, 'that we can't even get the drinks we want. Some bartender he is.'

Marshall opened his mouth to reply, but then his gaze shifted past her, and in the next moment she heard Lisa's voice coming from directly behind her.

'Darling,' she said to her husband, 'you're doing a simply marvellous job. I don't know what I'd do without you.'

Charles only glared at her and handed Jessica her drink. As she reached for it, she felt Lisa put a hand on her arm and bend down to speak to her.

'Jessica, there's someone here I want you to meet, dear.' Jessica turned then to face her, a polite smile on her face, bracing herself for yet another introduction to one of Lisa's many friends. Then she went rigid as she recognised the tall dark man behind Lisa.

'This is Jason Strong,' said Lisa. 'Jason, my sister-in-law, Jessica Carpenter.'

CHAPTER SEVEN

JESSICA felt as though all the breath had suddenly been knocked out of her. The smile on her face seemed pasted on, held there only by the sheerest reflex muscular spasm. Her hands gripped her drink so tightly she was afraid she would break the delicate crystal, and her mouth felt so dry that she simply couldn't speak a word.

'You two should have a lot in common,' Lisa was happily prattling on. 'Jason was in the revolution at the same time you were, Jessica. They thought he was a spy. Can you imagine? Actually, he's quite a famous reporter. Well, much more than a reporter, a journalist, really. Surely you've heard of him.'

Jessica could only stare, mesmerised, as Jason inclined his dark head briefly toward her. 'How do you do, Dr Carpenter?' he said gravely. 'Charles and Lisa have told me so much about you that I feel we've already met.'

Thank God, Jessica breathed, he's not going to mention our past relationship or that we knew each other at all down there. She could feel her tight shoulder muscles unclench themselves and her fingers relax their hold on the glass, as the tension slowly began to drain out of her.

'How do you do, Mr Strong,' she said politely. 'Of course, I know you by reputation.'

'You two will have to get together,' Lisa went on, 'and compare notes on your harrowing adventures.' She glanced up at Marshall. 'And, of course, you, too,

Marshall. Isn't it an amazing coincidence that all three of you were down there at the same time?'

Marshall, as though sensing Jessica's distress, had put a hand on her shoulder during the introductions. Although she wasn't too pleased with the way the possessive gesture implied a more intimate relationship between them than actually existed, she did feel profoundly grateful for his solid presence just behind her. It gave her not only a sense of security, but a measure of protection against the disturbing man who stood before her.

'How are you, Strong?' she heard Marshall say as he reached an arm out past Jessica to shake Jason's hand. 'Just back from Lebanon, aren't you?'

'That's right,' Jason replied. He darted an enigmatic glance at Jessica. 'I went there right after I left San Cristobal. I'm home on a sabbatical for now. I only arrived back yesterday.'

The two men began discussing the political situation in San Cristobal, technicalities and personalities that Jessica had largely ignored during her stay there. As they chatted, she felt her shaky equilibrium slowly returning and couldn't resist a few tentative glances at Jason. She had been so startled to see him here in her brother's apartment, the last place she would have expected, that she hadn't really taken in his dramatically changed appearance at first.

The man she had known in San Cristobal had seemed so rough to her, almost like an outlaw. She remembered the first night she had seen him at her door, his filthy clothes stained with blood from his wound, unshaven, wild-eyed. Then, later, during his convalescence, he had worn only the tattered rags she had found in the cupboard, left by the previous tenant. The man who stood before her now, chatting with Marshall so casually, was as different from the one she had known as it was possible to be: a polished man of the world, as confident in society as he was hiding out in the mountains. His dark suit fitted him to perfection, and the white dress shirt was dazzling against his deeply tanned face. If anything, she thought, with a tinge of regret, he was more devastating than ever.

It was then that she noticed the redheaded woman in the emerald green dress whom she had seen with Jason at the ball. She was clutching his arm tightly and holding herself closely up against his side. She eyed Jessica with patent distaste and made a face.

'Were you down in that terrible country, too?' she asked in a husky drawl.

Jessica gazed at her coolly, in full possession of herself once again now that Jason had made it clear he had no intention of resurrecting their past connection.

'It's not a terrible country at all,' she said a little more sharply than she had intended. 'It's a very poor, very troubled country, but it's quite beautiful, and the people are wonderful.'

Jason's eyes glinted briefly in amusement, and he turned to his companion. 'Dr Carpenter wasn't there as a tourist, Dorothy,' he said indulgently. 'She was working.'

Jessica couldn't miss the note of intimacy in his voice as he spoke to the beautiful redhead. She wondered who she was. She looked familiar, but she couldn't quite place her.

'Oh, I'm so sorry,' Lisa broke in. 'I've forgotten my manners. Jessica, this is Dorothy Davis. I don't believe you've met.' She turned to the redhead. 'My sister-in-law, Dorothy—Jessica Carpenter.'

The two women murmured polite acknowledgments of the introduction. At the mention of her full name, Jessica recognised her instantly as the daughter of a prominent cabinet member and, she recalled, the heiress-presumptive to a vast Oklahoma oil fortune. Her photograph appeared regularly in the society pages of Washington newspapers.

While Lisa introduced Marshall to Dorothy Davis, Jessica took a grateful sip of her drink and just sat listening to the conversation buzzing around her. Apparently, Marshall knew Dorothy's father quite well from one of his previous diplomatic postings, and they had several acquaintances in common.

Although she couldn't bring herself to look at him, she was intensely aware of Jason's dark gaze fastened on her. The worst is over, she told herself. We've met as strangers. I can leave soon, and I'll never have to see him again. She found that if she held on to that thought firmly, she could keep her balance and stay calm, at least on the surface.

'I understand you've set up practice already,' she heard him say to her.

He had moved in a little closer and spoke in a low tone. Still, the sound of his voice made her jump a little. She slowly raised her glass to her lips again, took another sip, then looked up at him, not quite meeting his eyes.

'That's right,' she said.

'Just as you'd planned.'

She gave him a sharp glance and nodded curtly. 'Yes,' she said in a clipped tone. 'Just as I'd planned.'

He leaned over and reached in front of her to set his own glass on the bar, almost touching her in the process. She moved back slightly on her stool to avoid contact with him, but he was so close to her now, his face turned in profile to her, that she could smell his distinctive clean masculine scent, see the long dark lashes resting on his high bony cheeks. A sharp jab of sudden longing caught at her heart, and it took a real effort to stop herself from reaching out and touching that familiar face. He needs a haircut, as usual, she thought crazily, and yearned to run her fingers up into the thick black hair that fell across his forehead.

Then he turned, his face quite close to hers, and forced her to meet his penetrating gaze. As her eyes met his, she noticed once again how variable the colour was. Tonight they were so dark as to appear almost violet, and she winced inwardly as she recalled that they always turned that colour under the pressure of emotion.

'I've got to talk to you, Jess,' he said in a voice so low that she could barely hear him.

For a moment she was tempted, but only for a moment. The hurt was still too fresh in her mind. It would be madness to resume any kind of involvement with this man, and she knew it.

'I don't think so, Jason,' she said calmly. 'We really have nothing to say to each other.'

He frowned, his eyebrows knitted together, and set his mouth in a hard line. He gave her a long appraising look, then, to her surprise, he smiled thinly and the gaze softened.

'You're angry,' he said. 'I was afraid of that.'

'Why, Jason,' she said through clenched teeth. 'What reason do I have to be angry?'

'Why don't you tell me?' he shot back at her.

She was about to elaborate those reasons, but she caught herself just in time as the meaning of his sudden smile dawned on her. Of course. He was pleased to see her angry. It was an emotional response, and if he could still arouse emotion in her, it meant that he still had power over her.

She managed to smile at him then. 'But I have nothing to tell,' she said. 'I'm just very busy these days.'

He gave her one swift disbelieving look, but she held her ground, kept smiling, and in a moment was intensely gratified to see his face fall.

'I see,' he said grimly. He laughed, a short dry bark. 'What happened between us in San Cristobal meant nothing. It was just a pleasant way to pass the revolution. Is that it?'

She lost it, then. How dared he accuse her of such a thing when he had meant the world to her and then had abandoned her with only that brief, cruel farewell note? She felt her temper rising out of control. Her face grew hot, her hands started to tremble.

'You bastard!' she said in a voice throbbing with emotion. '*You* walked out on *me*, if you recall!'

When she saw the slow, self-satisfied smile spread across his lean face, she realised instantly that she had made a dreadful mistake in letting him goad her into admitting her anger. Her only hope was to get him out of her life, her mind, her heart, for ever.

'You're very clever, Jason,' she said at last. 'Far too clever for me.' She slid off the stool and stood before him. 'But what I said before still goes. I don't ever want to see you again. Make of it what you will.'

She whirled around then and walked over to Marshall's side. He was still in the small group speaking with Lisa, Dorothy and Charles. She put her arm through his and clung to it as though it were a life preserver thrown to a drowning person.

Pleased, he glanced down at her with a smile and

covered her hand with his. 'Are you ready to go?' he asked. 'Or have you decided to stay the night?'

'No,' she said firmly. 'I don't want to stay. Let's sneak out now before Lisa notices.'

A quick glance showed her that Lisa was still deep in animated conversation with Dorothy Davis, her back turned. Charles was standing alone with his hands in his pockets, looking bored and tired. As Jessica walked quickly to his side, she could see out of the corner of her eye that Jason was still standing at the bar where she had left him.

'Charles,' she said when she reached him, 'I think I'll go on home after all.' She raised her head to give him a quick peck on the cheek. 'Tell Lisa, will you, so she won't worry about me.'

'You're sure?' he asked with a worried frown.

She gave him a reassuring smile. 'It's only a short drive.'

'Well, all right, then.' He yawned deeply, then covered it with his hand. 'Sorry,' he muttered, 'but I'm beat. Think I'll turn in myself.'

'They'll be leaving soon,' she consoled him. 'Good night, then. Thanks for everything.'

Without a glance towards the bar to see if Jason was still standing there, she hurried away from Charles towards Marshall, who was patiently waiting for her at the archway that led out into the foyer. As she made her way through the dwindling crowd, smiling her brief good nights, she had the overpowering sensation that a pair of brooding dark eyes was following her every step of the way.

It wasn't until she had retrieved her car and said good night to Marshall at the darkened, deserted French Embassy, and was driving home alone that she allowed herself to ponder the unexpected encounter that night with Jason Strong.

As she reconstructed the events of the evening in her mind, she was aware of only one consuming emotion, and that was an intense, all-encompassing rage. She found her hands gripping the steering wheel so tightly her fingers ached, and she was literally grinding her teeth at the thought of the man who had hurt her so badly.

'The arrogant, conceited *bastard*!' she cried aloud as she swung on to the beltway.

What did he expect? she asked herself, seething. That I would fall into his arms at the first sight of his irresistible presence? That we would just resume an affair that gave him everything he wanted, but would leave me hanging again the minute he decided to go off on one of his stupid stories?

She knew she wasn't being quite fair. She herself had allowed Jason his freedom all through their short liaison. It had seemed important to her then not to try to pin him down, to take one day at a time and not to worry about tomorrow.

The trouble was, she thought, that tomorrow never came. She would have let him go—not happily, but with grace and dignity—if he had given her the chance. It was the way he had sneaked out on her that was unforgivable, as though he was afraid she would make a scene or cling to him if he said goodbye to her.

As she got off the freeway and began driving slowly through the silent streets of Taunton towards her house, the stinging tears finally came. Her fury spent, a profound sadness and sense of loss swept over her. No matter what he was, she thought, wiping her eyes with the back of her hand, I loved him. And he knew it.

By the time she had parked the Thunderbird in the garage, gone inside and got ready for bed, she felt much better. Gratified, she got into bed and switched off the lamp. As she settled back on to the pillows with a deep sigh of relief, she felt she had passed an important milestone.

It was bound to happen, she told herself. I don't know what made me think I'd never see him again. It's better that I did. It was bad, but I did live through it. Now I can let him go for good.

She spent the next day raking the last of the leaves and pruning back the sprawling shrubbery just outside the bay window at the front of the dining-room. The house looked a little shabby, she thought. Maybe in the spring she would have it painted. One of the rain gutters in the back was leaking, too, and would need repair soon.

That afternoon, she built a fire in the living-room, made herself a pot of tea and settled down to glance through the voluminous Sunday paper. It had been a quiet, productive day, she thought with a glow of satisfaction. The few times she had found her thoughts straying to Jason Strong she had refused to allow herself to dwell on them. She had been quite firm with herself and managed to push them away. In time, she was convinced, they would vanish altogether.

Before she had taken her first sip of tea, the telephone in the hall started ringing. For a moment she was tempted not to answer it. When she first came to Taunton, Dr Weatherby had advised her to get an unlisted number. All professional calls went through the answering service, who wouldn't ring her unless it was an emergency.

It rang again, and still she debated. Dr Weatherby was on call this weekend, so it shouldn't be a patient. She had only given her private number to a very few people. Marshall had found it out, but then Lisa would have given it to him, knowing how helpful he had been to her in getting out of San Cristobal.

On the fourth ring, she decided she had better answer it. It was probably Lisa calling to scold her for ducking out of the party last night without saying good night. Grumbling a little to herself, she went out into the hall, wondering what it was that was so compelling about an insistently ringing telephone. One felt almost obliged to answer it.

It was still ringing when she picked it up.

'Hello.'

'Jessica? It's Jason.'

She couldn't speak. Her hand gripped the telephone tighter and slowly she sank into the chair next to the stand. There was an unpleasant tight sensation in her throat, and a most peculiar ringing in her ears.

'How did you get my number?' she said curtly.

'I have ways of finding out those things. I'm a reporter, remember?'

'How could I forget?'

'Look, Jess, I've got to talk to you. I need to explain why I did what I did in San Cristobal, why I left so abruptly. If you'll just give me a chance . . .'

'Listen, Jason, I said it last night, and I'll say it again. I don't want to see you or talk to you, not ever again. Leave me alone. Go and play with Dorothy What's-Her-Name.'

'God, you're stubborn,' he said in an exasperated tone. 'I'm coming out there, and you're going to listen to me if I have to . . .'

'Now, you listen to me, Jason Strong, and listen

well. If you come here, I won't open the door. If you persist, I'll call the police. I know it's unbelievable to a man of your conceit, but I don't want any part of you. I'm going to hang up now. Goodbye.'

There, she thought with satisfaction, as she cradled the receiver quietly back in position. That should do it. The nerve, she thought, as she went back to the fire, the utter, unbelievable nerve of the man! Before she could sit down, the phone rang again. She made a face, hesitated, then decided to ignore it. He would get sick of it before long.

For the next hour it rang regularly every fifteen minutes, until finally, exasperated, she marched back out into the hall, muttering along the way that this was harassment, and wondering if she would have to change her number again.

'Listen,' she snarled into the receiver, 'this has got to stop!'

'Jessica?' came Lisa's voice. 'Stop what? I've been calling and calling. Are you all right?'

Jessica had to laugh. She sat down on the chair, weak with relief. 'I'm sorry, Lisa; I've been getting some crank calls lately. What's on your mind?'

'I just wanted to make sure you got home all right,' Lisa said in a hurt tone.

'Yes, Lisa, of course I got home all right. You shouldn't worry about me so. After all, if I can survive a revolution, surely I can make my way to Taunton from Washington.'

'Well, I do worry about you. I was telling Charles just the other day that you don't seem like your old self since you've been back.'

'I was gone a year, Lisa,' she explained patiently. 'People do change in a year.'

'Yes, but . . .'

'A lot happened to me down there, Lisa,' she interrupted. 'It was a pretty exciting and harrowing experience, and it will take me a while to settle back down into a normal routine again.'

'Are you sure that's all? I thought you seemed quite upset last night when I introduced you to Jason Strong.'

Jessica gripped the phone tighter and slowly rose to her feet. At all costs, she had to keep her past relationship with that man buried. Could Lisa have guessed something?

'Upset?' she asked weakly, stalling for time.

'Yes, upset,' came the firm reply. 'I talked it over with Charles later, but you know men, especially your brother. They don't notice anything really important. Anyway, we finally decided that he must have reminded you of something awful that happened down there, something you've buried in your unconscious. Even though you'd never actually met him before, still he was down there at the same time, and meeting him may have triggered off a memory you've repressed.'

Jessica had to smile. A few years ago Lisa, with too much time and energy on her hands, had taken a course in psychology at Georgetown. Ever since, it had become a hobby of hers to analyse all her friends' idiosyncrasies, and her favourite diagnosis was a repressed trauma wreaking havoc in the unconscious.

Jessica decided the safest course was to play along with her. 'You might be right, Lisa.' Actually, even though she was way off base in her reasoning, there was a grain of truth in it. 'I'll give it serious thought.'

'That's good, dear,' Lisa said, apparently mollified, 'and if you ever need to talk it over, I'm always available to listen.' She hesitated, then said. 'I *do* worry about you.'

'Honestly, Lisa, there's no need!' Lisa could be exasperating, she thought, but still, her concern was clearly genuine.

'Charles and I both like Marshall very much,' her sister-in-law said.

Jessica knew that this apparently abrupt change of subject was misleading. Somehow, Lisa's concern and her approval of Marshall were connected.

'I do, too,' she said cautiously.

'He's obviously smitten with you, dear.'

'Now, Lisa, don't go building anything in your mind over a casual friendship.'

'My intuition tells me it could be more than that if you wanted it to be. He's a marvellous catch, Jessica, just ripe for settling down.'

Just then, the doorbell rang. Saved by the bell, Jessica thought. The conversation was getting sticky.

'There's someone at the door, Lisa,' she said hurriedly. 'I'll talk to you later.'

It wasn't until she'd hung up and started towards the front door that she remembered Jason's threatened intention to come out to Taunton to see her. She hesitated. Would she really call the police if he wouldn't go? Finally, she decided to peek out through the living-room window, which offered a clear view of the front door. If she hid behind the curtains, he wouldn't see her. If it was Jason, she decided, she just wouldn't answer the door. And if he persisted, she *would* call the police. It would serve him right.

But when she pulled the curtain aside to see who it was, she was taken somewhat aback at the sight of Mr Thorson from next door. 'That's good,' she muttered to herself, as she went to see what he wanted, but even so, she couldn't deny the little jab of disappointment the minute she'd realised it wasn't Jason after all.

It was while she was standing on the steps talking to Mr Thorson, who wanted her to sign a petition for a local leash law, that the strange car pulled up at the kerb. It was one she had never seen before, dark silvery-grey in colour, and it looked foreign.

Somehow she knew, even before he got out and started marching determinedly up the front path, that it would be Jason. She couldn't escape now, even if she wanted to, and to tell the truth, her curiosity was aroused by his single-minded pursuit. It might be interesting—entertaining, at least—to hear what he had to say.

With half her attention, she listened to her neighbour angrily expounding on the depredations wrought by the wandering dogs of the neighbourhood to his petunia bed, but the other half was fixed firmly on Jason.

He had stopped halfway to the door to examine the piles of leaves she had raked, just as though he owned the place, she thought furiously. It would serve him right if she ran inside, bolted the door and called the police, as she had threatened.

On the other hand, what, really, had he done that she could accuse him of? 'Please, officer, arrest this man for breaking my heart.' Put that way, it sounded pretty silly. Besides, he didn't seem nearly so threatening to her today as he had last night. The sun was shining, the cool air clear and crisp, and above all, she was on her own territory.

'Well, Jessica,' Mr Thorson was saying in an annoyed tone, 'will you sign it or not?'

'Yes, of course, Mr Thorson. Just show me where.'

Anything, she thought, to get rid of him.

As she signed her name in the place on the petition where he indicated, she was aware that Jason was slowly continuing on towards the house now. In just a few seconds he would be there, confronting her. Certain now that she could handle him, she wished only that she wasn't dressed in her worn blue jeans and paint-stained sweatshirt. She felt at a slight disadvantage knowing she didn't look her best, especially when he was so well turned out.

She still couldn't get over the change in him from the unkempt, shabbily dressed outlaw hiding from the soldiers in San Cristobal to this confident-looking man in the dark grey flannel trousers, navy-blue blazer and crisp white dress shirt.

Just as he reached the door, Mr Thorson, his objective attained at last, turned to go, and the two men almost collided. They nodded briefly at each other, then Mr Thorson hurried down the path to the street, obviously anxious to get his precious petition filled before nightfall.

'Hello, Jason,' she said when they were alone.

He stood before her, unsmiling, his hands shoved in his trousers pockets. The setting sun was behind him, casting bright glints through his thick black hair, and for a moment her confidence wavered. Why does he have to be so darned attractive? she thought. Why do I still, after all that's happened, find him so appealing?

'Can I come in?' he said at last. 'I'd like to talk to you.'

She thought a minute, then, reluctantly said, 'All right, Jason. For a few minutes.'

As he followed her in through the front door and she shut it behind her, she had a brief moment of panic at the thought that now they were inside the house alone together. Yet, she told herself, she'd have to face it sooner or later, and she might as well get it over with now. Jason Strong was not the kind of man to give up once he had determined on a course of action.

She would be polite, but distant, she decided. She would listen to him calmly, hear what he had to say, then send him packing. She wouldn't get emotional. No anger, no accusations, no threats. But when he was through, she would make it absolutely clear to him that that was it, that she never wanted to see him or talk to him again.

'Would you like a cup of tea?' she asked when they reached the living-room. 'I'm afraid it's cold by now, but I could heat it up. Or I could give you a drink. I don't usually stock much alcohol, but . . .'

'Nothing, thanks,' he broke in abruptly.

They were standing in front of the fire, some three feet apart. While she was chattering on about the tea, she had looked everywhere but at him. Now, however, his sharp tone startled her, and, wide-eyed, she met his gaze.

'I came to talk,' he said in a gentler tone, 'not to be entertained.' His glance travelled around the room, taking it all in. 'This is quite pleasant,' he said at last. 'Very homey. Just what you wanted.'

What I wanted, she felt like screaming at him, was to be with you. Anywhere in the world. He was making it sound as though she had left him because of his dangerous life-style instead of the other way around, and it was on the tip of her tongue to lash out at him, to point out the actual facts of their parting, but she stopped herself just in time, reminding herself of her vow not to get emotional.

'I like it,' was all she said. 'Why don't we sit down?'

He made an impatient gesture in the air, frowned and took a step forwards. It was all she could do to keep herself from shrinking back from him. The civilised man in the conservative clothes suddenly appeared to her to be reverting to the outlaw of the mountains.

'I didn't come here for polite chit-chat or a tea party,' he said in a harsh tone.

Her heart caught in her throat at the sight of this wilder Jason, but she stood her ground, and although her hands were clenched into tight fists at her side, she managed to give a proud lift to her chin as she faced him.

'Why did you come, then, Jason? What do we have to say to each other?'

He stared at her for a long time, the heavy lids half lowered over his steely eyes. The tension in the silent room was electric. Jessica had the eerie sensation that something far more significant than her relationship with Jason Strong was at stake here. Something about his tone, his whole attitude towards her, seemed to challenge and threaten the very depths of her being.

'How can you ask such a question?' he said in a low voice. 'After what happened between us, do you seriously suggest we have nothing to say to each other?'

Her heart gave a great leap in her breast. He was deadly serious. Was it possible that he really had cared about her after all? Then she remembered that awful farewell note, the beautiful Dorothy Davis clinging to him last night, and a surge of resentment swept over her.

'I'd like to remind you, Jason,' she said in a voice

almost trembling with suppressed anger, 'that you were the one who cared so little about what happened between us that you left me without even saying goodbye. That touching note you left me could have been written to a mere acquaintaince or even a servant.'

To her horror, as the whole humiliating episode came rushing into her mind again, she heard her voice break and felt the hot tears sting her eyes. She hated to have him see her weakness, but she couldn't help herself. She watched, unable to move, as he spread his hands in a helpless gesture, then moved swiftly forwards.

She immediately sensed the danger in him, and before he could reach her or touch her, she stepped back, her mind firmly made up that not to resist him now would be the end of her security forever.

'No!' she cried. 'Don't come near me! Don't touch me! That won't work any more.'

He stopped short and stood glaring down at her, just inches away. She could tell that he was struggling to control his own temper, but she would not allow her gaze to falter. Finally, with a lift of his broad shoulders, he turned and walked over to the fire, still blazing in the hearth. He stood there for a long time staring down at the flickering flames, then slowly turned to face her again.

'All right, Jess. Have it your way,' he said wearily. 'I'll speak my piece, then if you still want me to go, I will.' He gave her an enquiring look, but she remained silent, and in a moment he began to speak in a low voice. 'I guess I handled my departure badly, looking back on it, but at the time it seemed like the only thing I could do. I've been in enough internal squabbles in countries just like San Crístobal to know that the lull in the fighting was only temporary. I had two things on my mind: to get you safely out of the country while the cease-fire was in effect, and to get my story.'

He stopped for a moment and looked at her questioningly. The flickering firelight cast shadows on his lean, dark face, and the sheer beauty of the man almost took her breath away. When she didn't speak, he took a breath and went on.

'I was afraid that if you knew I was staying in the country to get my story, you wouldn't leave. What was I to do? You tell me. Maybe I was wrong. What if I had stayed to say goodbye to you and told you to leave without me? Would you have gone?'

She still didn't trust herself to speak. She felt absolutely torn in two. Part of her yearned to throw herself into his arms, to resume their relationship where they had left off, but another part, the sensible part, told her that to do so would mean no turning back. She would be set irrevocably on a dangerous course she could have no hope of controlling.

He stood just inches away, waiting for her to speak. When she remained silent, the concerned look on his face slowly changed into a puzzled frown, then a red flush began to spread over his neck up into the flat planes of his cheeks.

'You don't believe me,' he said at last in a flat tone.

Do I believe him? she asked herself. She didn't know. It didn't even seem important any more. Her one thought was to be free of his disturbing presence. Even now, watching him, she could feel desire beginning to well up in her, and if she were to give in to it, she knew beyond the shadow of a doubt that she would be lost.

'It doesn't matter,' she said dully. 'Perhaps you

were only thinking about my welfare. I'm willing to give you the benefit of the doubt and say you were. But it doesn't change anything.'

'Would you care to explain that?' he asked carefully.

She raised her chin defiantly. 'I don't have to explain anything to you, Jason. I have a perfect right to tell you simply that I don't want you in my life.'

'I don't believe you.'

'Believe what you like. I've let you in my house, I've listened to you, I probably believe you're telling me the truth about why you left the way you did. Now I want you to go. I don't ever want to see you or hear from you again.'

She saw his shoulders slump, then a look of ineffable weariness descend on his features, and for one brief moment she wanted to go to him, to tell him she didn't mean any of it, that she still loved him and was willing to accept him on any terms.

He shook his head slowly. 'I had no idea I'd hurt you so badly,' he said sadly. 'I thought I was doing the right thing.'

'Please go,' she whispered.

'All right, I'll go now.' He turned and strode away from her towards the front door. Before stepping into the hall, he stopped and turned around and fixed her with a long look. 'But I'm not giving up.'

With that he was gone.

CHAPTER EIGHT

WHEN Jason was gone, Jessica stood there in the middle of the room, her body rigid, her fists still clenched at her sides, listening to the front door open and close, his footsteps fading away as he went down the path, and finally the roar of his engine as he drove away.

Then she stumbled to the couch, put her head in her hands and groaned aloud. The tense emotional scene had left her shattered and drained of energy.

After a while, she switched on the lamp beside the couch and reached for the untouched pot of tea on the table. It was stone cold by now. She stood up and carried it into the kitchen, thinking she would heat it. Instead, when she got there, she poured it out into the sink and reached for the bottle of sherry up in the cupboard.

She filled her teacup with it and took a long swallow. The wine warmed her, and slowly her frayed nerves began to mend. She finished her wine, rinsed out the cup, then leaned against the draining-board to gaze out of the window at the darkening sky. Heavy clouds were blowing in from the south, obscuring the moon and stars. It would rain before morning.

I've either done the stupidest thing in my life, she thought, or the wisest, and I simply don't know which. I still want him, she had to admit to herself. Oh, how I want him! And I do believe him. He was thinking of me. Of course I wouldn't have left if I

127

thought I could be with him.

And then what? He had said himself at the party last night that he'd gone straight to Lebanon from San Cristobal. What would she have done then? Stuck in that war-torn country, possibly missing her last chance to get out—and without Jason anyway.

No, she told herself firmly as she switched on the kitchen light and took down a can of soup for her supper, I did the right thing, the only possible thing. My life is here, now, where I'm safe. There can't possibly be a future for me with Jason Strong. He'll never change. He thrives on danger and adventure. I was right to send him away.

She was so busy during the following week that the entire episode began gradually to fade from her mind until she could almost believe it had never happened, that he hadn't reappeared in her life at all.

At first, she half expected him to pursue the matter, and was surprised when she heard nothing from him. She was also, perversely, disappointed. His parting words to her were that he was not giving up. Apparently he had changed his mind. It wasn't like him to let go of something he really wanted, and she could only conclude that he had decided she wasn't worth the bother, especially with a woman like Dorothy Davis—rich, beautiful, obviously adoring him—to soothe his wounded masculine pride.

She still thought about him. She knew she always would. Such a man was not easily forgotten, but as the days passed her conviction that she had acted wisely in sending him away only grew stronger.

Her practice picked up dramatically as Dr Weatherby began referring more and more of his patients to her and they overcame their initial reservations about being treated by a woman doctor. She was especially pleased to find that more and more men were coming to her for help, bypassing Dr Weatherby entirely.

What really marked the seal of acceptance to her was when, on Friday, a brawny young construction worker allowed her to set his broken leg. It was touch and go at first. Even though he was in terrible pain from the multiple fracture, she couldn't miss the look of alarm on his face when she entered the small consulting-room where his friends had laid him on the table.

'Where's Doc Weatherby?' he barked at her between groans.

'Today's his day off,' she said calmly as she bent over him and started examining his leg. She turned to Mrs Schultz, the grey-haired nurse. 'I'll need some scissors and an ampoule of Demerol.'

'What do you need scissors for?' the young man cried, as though his very masculinity was threatened. He raised himself up on his elbows, then gave a yelp of pain and flopped his head back down.

She put a hand on his damp forehead and brushed the mop of curly blonde hair back in a soothing gesture.

'It's just to cut off your trouser leg,' she said with a smile. 'Don't worry. I really do know what I'm doing. Now, I'm going to give you something for the pain, then take an x-ray so I'll know better what you've done to yourself.'

He looked up at her, wavering, but still wary. 'You're sure you're a doctor?' He forced out a crooked grin. 'You're too pretty to be a real doctor.'

She nodded firmly and picked up the hypodermic needle. 'Absolutely. That's the way they make them these days. You just relax, now, and in a minute you'll feel better.'

She deftly jabbed the needle into his vein, then set to work to cut away the torn dirty jeans that covered his leg. She worked quickly and efficiently, and a half-hour later his leg was in a cast, and he was practising with his crutches.

'Don't get the cast wet,' she said sternly as his friends ushered him out the door, 'and don't put any weight on it. It'll take about six weeks to heal, but I'll want to check that cast once a week. You can arrange it with Mrs Schultz.'

'Okay, Doc,' he said cheerfully. At the door he turned and grinned at her. 'And thanks. For a lady doctor, you're okay.'

'I'll take that as a compliment,' she said drily, shooing him off.

And why not? she asked herself as she watched him hobble off down the hall toward the reception-room. Medicine was a field that was ideally suited for a woman. Unlike the law or business, where it was necessary to adopt a more ruthless spirit in order to compete with men, all it took to be a good doctor was an education and a sense of caring.

'What's next?' she asked Mrs Schultz when she returned.

The older woman gave her an appraising glance. 'Why don't you take a break, Doctor? Have a cup of coffee. It's been a long day for you; you must be tired.'

Jessica gave the nurse a grateful smile. 'I'm all right—but thanks anyway.'

Mrs Schultz shrugged her heavy shoulders. 'Suit yourself. But if you don't mind a piece of advice, you've got to learn to pace yourself. You don't have to prove anything. You're a good doctor,' she added stiffly, 'and I should know. I've worked with the best and the worst of 'em for thirty years.' She nodded abruptly. 'You're okay.'

Ah, Jessica thought with satisfaction as she watched the nurse move on to the next examination-room and pull the chart clipped to the door. High praise, indeed! She really had arrived if the taciturn Mrs Schultz finally approved of her.

Her next patient was a young pregnant woman in her final month who only needed a routine check-up. This was Jessica's favourite kind of patient, one bringing life into the world. It gave a real lift to her spirits, and when she was through, her tiredness seemed to have evaporated.

Next was poor arthritic Mrs Columbo, who had developed a severe anaemia that had Jessica serious-ly worried. She was such a thin, frail little thing.

'You must eat properly,' she told the shrunken old lady patiently. 'Liver, fish, lean meat.'

Mrs Columbo made a face and shook her head sadly from side to side. 'I can't, Doctor.' She patted her stomach. 'Those things make me sick.'

Jessica sighed. 'All right, I'll write you a prescrip-tion for some high-potency iron tablets, but just to get you started, I'm going to have Mrs Schultz give you a shot. She's very good at it,' she rushed on when she saw the frightened look on the old lady's lined face. 'Nurses are far better at it than doctors.'

She went out into the corridor and called the nurse. After she had explained what she wanted her to do, she glanced at her watch. It was after five o'clock.

'Is that it for the day, Mrs Schultz?' She suddenly felt very tired again. Poor Mrs Columbo had depressed her profoundly.

'One more, Doctor,' she said briskly. 'Then you can go home and get some rest.' She handed Jessica the chart. 'It's a new patient, in number four. A possible heart problem.'

Jessica glanced briefly at the chart as she walked slowly down the hall to the number four waiting-room. She only hoped it wasn't a serious problem. Most people who worried about their hearts were actually suffering from indigestion, she had found, but you never knew until you checked it out thoroughly. There were also the people who thought they just had stomach cramps only to suffer a severe coronary a few hours later.

She stepped inside the small examination room. A man was sitting on the edge of the table, stripped to the waist, his back towards her. She started to read his chart more closely.

'Well, Mr Smith, I understand you're having a problem with your heart. What seems to be the trouble?'

'I think it's broken,' came a low, familiar voice.

She could feel the blood rushing out of her face as it dawned on her that the man sitting there was Jason Strong. She raised her eyes slowly from the chart and stared at him. He had twisted his upper body around to face her, a quizzical half-smile on his face.

'You!' she breathed, hardly able to believe her eyes. This was the last place she had expected to see him. 'What are you doing here?'

He shrugged. 'It was all I could think of. I knew you'd only hang up if I called you and wouldn't let me in your house if I showed up there. I figured you'd have to talk to me in here.'

Her first impulse was to lash out at him furiously, and she even opened her mouth to do just that, but the angry words died on her lips. He looked so wonderful to her, sitting there with the sinuous grace of an athlete, his tanned chest and shoulders bare, that she simply couldn't help herself.

'Oh, Jason,' she said with a sigh. 'What am I going to do with you?'

He slid off the edge of the table and strode towards her. 'Why don't you take me home with you? I purposely asked for the last appointment of the day so that you could do just that.'

She bit her lip and frowned up at him. 'I don't know, Jason. What's the point? We don't really have anything to talk about.'

'I'm not going to let you go,' he said firmly. He placed one palm flat on his smooth chest. 'As a doctor, would you want to be responsible for a broken heart? That could kill a person, you know.'

She had to smile. He looked so comical standing there, half-naked, a pathetic look on his face, and so totally, completely irresistible. It suddenly occurred to her for the first time since she had let him into her house, and her heart, that night down in the village, that she had a measure of power over him.

The thought stunned her. From the beginning, she had been so bowled over by the sheer magnetism of the man, so overwhelmed by the dormant passion he had awakened in her, that she had automatically assumed that all the power in their relationship lay in his hands. She had given it to him gladly, even basing all her future plans on his. It had simply never occurred to her that he might bend to her will. The thought elated her, but in the next second, when she saw the responsibility of such a power, she sobered immediately.

'What do you want from me, Jason?'

A light appeared in the deep-grey eyes. 'Right now I want to get my clothes back on. Then I want you to let me come home with you so we can talk. Will you do that for me, Jess? It's important to me that you at least listen to what I have to say. Then, if you still want me out of your life, I'll go, and I won't bother you again. Will you do it?'

She crossed her arms in front of her and gave him a stern look. 'Well, since you've gone to so much trouble, Mr *Smith*, I guess that's the least I can do.'

'Thank you,' he said.

'Why don't you get dressed and wait for me out in front. I'll only be a few minutes.'

'All right,' he said. He turned and reached for his shirt, hanging over a chair.

'Wait a minute,' she said.

She put the stethoscope hanging around her neck on his chest, adjusted the earpieces, and listened to his thudding heartbeat for a few seconds.

'It sounds all right to me, Mr Smith. I don't think you have a thing to worry about. That's a good strong beat.'

'We'll see,' he said with an enigmatic smile, and reached his arms into his shirtsleeves.

It wasn't until he was gone and she was alone in the building that it struck her what she had done. After Jason left, she said good night to Mrs Schultz, then went back into her own tiny office to take off her white coat and collect her suit jacket and handbag. She stood there now listening to the quiet. No telephone rang, no frightened child wept, no suffering patient complained, just a dead, eerie silence.

She walked slowly into the lavatory to wash her hands and repair the ravages of the hectic day on her hair and make-up. As she gazed into the mirror over the sink, she had the odd, unsettling sensation that she was looking at a stranger.

'Are you out of your mind?' she muttered aloud to her reflection.

God, she thought, as she dried her hands, if only he weren't so appealing to her! Sure, she added, me and probably a hundred other women! She combed out her shoulder-length blonde hair and added a quick slash of lipstick to her mouth. With the improvement in her appearance, her confidence began to return.

She slipped on her jacket, snapped her bag shut and walked down the hall to the front entrance, turning out lights as she went. When she stepped outside and saw his car at the kerb, she faltered again. It was already starting to get dark, and she could barely make out the dim form sitting in the driver's seat. Then there was a sudden reddish glow as he struck a match, lit a cigarette and drew on it, and his lean face was briefly illuminated. The moment the familiar features came into view, she knew with a sudden certainty that it would be madness to be alone with this man in her house at night. He still had too much power over her.

Hurriedly, she turned and locked the front door of the office, then set her shoulders high and walked down the path to the waiting car, her heels tapping lightly on the pavement.

If I had any sense, she told herself as she went, I'd run as fast as I could in the opposite direction. She'd listen to him, though, as she'd promised, but that was all, and she vowed she would steel herself against any personal involvement. Her life was here. She liked it just the way it was. She was not going to allow Jason Strong to turn it upside down and then vanish again.

He had the engine going before she reached the

car, and when she got inside, she turned to him before he could make the U-turn that led back to her street.

'I've changed my mind, Jason,' she said firmly. 'I don't think it would be a good idea for you to come home with me.'

He raised an eyebrow. 'Afraid of what your dog-hating neighbour might say?'

She flushed deeply. 'Of course not. I just would feel more comfortable in a public place.'

He released the handbrake and the car moved forward. 'You mean you'd feel safer, don't you?'

'Don't flatter yourself,' she said curtly, but his observation had come too close to the truth to suit her. Then inspiration hit her. 'I just don't think it would be prudent since you're so involved with Dorothy Davis.'

He only darted her a brief sideways glance as he manoeuvred the car out into the sparse flow of traffic. As usual, his expression was unreadable, but something in it made her regret the rather juvenile comment.

'Well, where to, then?' he asked easily as he drove.

She searched her mind for a likely place that was public yet quiet, where they could have the talk he seemed so eager for and perhaps one quick drink. At the moment, a drink sounded like a very good idea, indeed. Taunton didn't offer much in the way of night life. Then she remembered The Willow Inn.

'I know a place,' she said, and told him how to get there.

They drove the few blocks to the inn in a stiff, unbroken silence. Glancing covertly at him from time to time, she could see only that he seemed relaxed as he drove, but stared ahead with a concentrated, brooding expression on his face, as though deep in thought. Manufacturing a good tale to tell me, she decided, but in the next moment she had to ask herself why he would bother. Why was he going to so much trouble?

The close intimacy of the car, along with the tense silence, only added to her discomfiture. She wondered what he was thinking; you never knew with him. Probably mulling over his latest newspaper story, she thought, and not thinking of her at all. She opened her mouth once to make an inane comment about the weather, then thought better of it and turned her head to gaze blindly out of the window.

She was so relieved when they reached the inn that she opened her door and jumped out on to the pavement the moment he pulled into the parking lot in front and shut off the engine. Then, of course, she had to stand there awkwardly and wait for him while he got out of the car on his side and strolled in a leisurely manner around to join her.

She was beginning to feel really annoyed. Why did he always manage to put her on the defensive like this? He made her feel like a naïve, gawky schoolgirl. I am a responsible adult, she reminded herself as they walked wordlessly towards the front entrance, and a qualified doctor. People entrust me with their lives. This man has no power over me except what I choose to give him.

He was the one who had hounded and tricked her into this meeting, after all. Why didn't he say something? Why go to all this trouble to seek her out and corner her if he was going to remain mute?

By the time they were seated at an isolated table in the very dim and near-deserted dining room, she was really angry. She was tired and hungry, and she didn't even want to discuss the past with a man who had no future to offer her, so what was she doing sitting here? The thing to do, she decided, was to tell him what he wanted to hear, that she believed every word of his cock-and-bull story, then ask him to take her home.

The waitress came just then to take their order, and before she left, she lit the candle in the centre of the table. When she was gone, Jessica glanced at Jason, ready to follow through on her decision, but the look on his face as the soft candlelight hit it stopped her. He was staring intently at her, and what she saw there was a naked supplication. The dark eyes were pleading, and he held his shoulders rigidly, as though in anticipation of a life or death battle.

'God, I've missed you, Jess,' he said.

It was a simple statement. He didn't reach across the table for her, he didn't move at all, he hardly seemed to be breathing. Her own breath caught in her throat as they sat there silently for several moments, their eyes locked together.

He looked so wonderful sitting there across from her, so strong and determined, yet at the same time so vulnerable, that she couldn't bear it. All her brave resolutions simply flew out of the window, and a great yearning, almost maternal in its intensity, filled her being. She could feel the tears welling up behind her eyes, and before she could stop them, slowly trickling down her cheeks.

'Don't cry, Jess,' he said in alarm. 'Please don't cry. You're my strong, brave girl.'

'I'm not crying,' she sobbed.

He only smiled at her, his eyes softened and dark with emotion. He pulled a clean handkerchief out of his jacket pocket and reached across the table to wipe her eyes.

'Of course you're not,' he said.

Her mind was thrown into total confusion. The last thing she had expected from him was this gentleness. The tears had been bad enough, especially when she had been so confident she could remain cool and detached. Now she didn't know what to think or how to act, and she was certainly in no condition to make a decision.

'Jess, the last thing in the world I wanted was to hurt you,' he went on earnestly. 'You must believe that. What we had together those few short weeks in San Cristobal meant the world to me. Perhaps I did wrong to leave the way I did, but at the same time it seemed the best thing to do for both of us. Can you honestly say that you would have left the country when you did if I'd stayed there with you?'

'No,' she whispered. She had to smile. 'In fact, I had it all planned out that you would leave with me, but I had also decided that if you wouldn't go, I'd stay, too. Then, when I thought you'd walked out on me . . .' Her voice trailed off.

'You left,' he said simply. 'And that's what I wanted. Your safety.'

The waitress brought their drinks just then. Jessica was grateful for the interruption, and while she set down the cocktail napkins, then the glasses, Jason silently handed Jessica the handkerchief. She took it gratefully and blew her nose as unobtrusively as possible.

While Jason was paying, she recovered herself enough to think more clearly, and she watched him across the table. The light was so dim that she couldn't accurately read his expression. Was he telling the truth? If so, he had cared far more deeply for her than she had imagined. Why would he lie?

Just to get her into bed again? That didn't make sense; he obviously had his pick of women. Not only that, but the way he lived, his dedication to his work, his love of danger, no one woman would ever mean so much to him that he would go to so much trouble just to resume a meaningless affair.

He was an enigma to her. She had never known anyone like him. So self-contained, so determined, almost ruthless in his pursuit of his vocation, totally unconcerned about the risks he ran, yet, on the other hand, so gentle with her just now, so anxious to make her understand why he had acted the way he did.

The waitress was gone now, and he turned his head to meet her gaze. 'Do you believe me, Jess?' he asked.

His low, urgent tone told her it was really important to him. Still she hesitated, not so much because she thought he was lying to her, but because she knew that much more hung on her answer than that.

'Yes, Jason,' she said at last. 'I believe you.'

The bluish-grey eyes deepened. An almost fierce light glinted in them as he gazed at her for a long time. She had the uncanny sensation that they were back in the village, that once again they were the only two people in the universe and time stood still.

He raised his glass in a salute, then took a long swallow. Then he gave her a stern look.

'Now, what's going on between you and Marshall Bennett?'

She sipped her drink slowly, stalling for time while she debated her answer. Her first instinct was to assure him immediately that Marshall was only a friend, but then she remembered Jason's appearance at the ball with Dorothy Davis, the very day after he arrived back in Washington from Lebanon, and decided to let him stew for a while. It would do him good.

'Why, Jason,' she said, setting her glass down. 'Don't tell me you're jealous?'

The dark eyes gleamed. 'You're damn right I'm jealous,' he said promptly and firmly. 'I didn't like the way he was pawing you.'

She raised her eyebrows in mock surprise. 'I don't see why that should bother you,' she said sweetly, 'when you had such a beautiful redhead to console you.'

He frowned and gave a slight snort of disgust. 'Dorothy's father is an old friend of mine,' he said in an annoyed tone. 'He called me the day I got back and asked me as a special favour to take her to that damned ball. I had planned to start tracking you down the very next day. Then, when Lisa asked us to her party and I knew you would be there, I just couldn't resist the opportunity.' He shrugged. 'Dorothy is not only spoiled rotten, she's also an empty-headed party girl. She means so little to me that I didn't even think how it might look to you to see us together.' He reached out and took her hand. 'You're all I care about, Jess. Only you.'

She felt as though she were melting inside, every defence shattered. This was what she had longed for. Jason cared about her! Nothing else mattered.

'Oh, Jason,' she said in a shaky voice, and couldn't go on.

The dining-room was beginning to fill up now as the supper crowd drifted in, and was growing noisier. In the background soft music was playing.

'Let's get out of here,' Jason said abruptly. His voice was gruff and slightly choked.

Without waiting for her reply, he released her

hand, pushed his chair back and stood up. He picked up some of the change the waitress had left and put it in his trousers pocket, then reached out his hand for her. She took it without a word and slowly rose from her seat.

It was quite dark out by now, with no sign of a moon. There was a definite nip in the damp night air, and as they started walking towards the car, he put his arm around her and held her closely up against him.

The minute they were inside the car, he turned to her and reached out for her. As his strong arms came around her, she yielded herself up to him gladly, and when he kissed her hair, her forehead, her face, her throat, she realised just how much she had missed him, longed for him, in spite of her anger.

Then his seeking mouth opened over hers, and one hand came down to settle possessively on her breast. At the touch, desire rose up in her like a consuming flame, and she reached out blindly for him. All her senses were alive to him, the taste of his mouth, the clean scent of his hair and skin, the touch of his hard body against hers and the warm hand on her breast.

He tore his mouth from hers and gripped her by the shoulders, holding her away from him a short distance and gazing down into her eyes. 'Let me come home with you, Jess,' he said hoarsely. 'Let me make love to you.'

There was a sudden blinding glare just then as another car came up behind them. It was only a momentary flash before the car pulled into the slot next to theirs, but enough to startle her into pulling away from him, out of his arms.

Several people emerged from the car alongside them, laughing and joking loudly. Doors slammed, and the voices faded as they moved off towards the inn. It was all over in a few seconds, but in that time, Jessica realised, in a brief flash of insight, that much as she still loved this man and as desperately as she wanted him, she couldn't just blindly hop into bed with him again. There couldn't possibly be a future with him. To resume their affair now would only mean more heartache for her later. He would leave her again the minute another dangerous assignment came along.

'Well?' he said when the others were gone. 'Shall we go?'

'Yes,' she replied. 'I think we'd better.' She turned to him. 'But I can't let you stay.'

He gave her a long, hard look. 'I don't understand,' he said at last in a flat tone. 'You said you believed me, and I know damned well you want me as much as I want you.'

'You're right,' she said sadly. There was no point in trying to deny it. He had seen for himself, just moments ago, how completely she had responded to his touch, his kiss.

'What's the problem, then?'

'Try to see it from my point of view for a moment, Jason,' she said gently. 'Suppose we do start again where we left off in San Cristobal. What then? Where do we go from there? I see nothing ahead for us—for me, at any rate—except another bitter disappointment when you leave me again.'

He didn't say anything for a long time. She sensed him move away from her and slump back in his seat, heard him light a cigarette and saw the deep frown on his lean face as the flash of the match briefly illuminated it.

'Still concerned about all the tomorrows?' he said at last.

'I have to be,' she said quietly. 'I'm the one who gets left. Your life is out there in the world,' she went on, waving an arm vaguely in the air. 'Mine is here. It's not possible for me to have any kind of life if you're going to be bouncing in and out of it all the time.'

'You want someone nice and safe, like Marshall Bennett,' he said bitterly.

'I have no interest in Marshall Bennett,' she said. Now was not the time to play games. She had to be absolutely truthful.

He crushed out his cigarette in the ashtray, then started the car and drove out of the car park into the street. Neither of them said a word on the way to her house. There was nothing to say, she thought miserably. It was an impossible situation.

When he pulled up at the kerb in front of her house, he switched off the engine and turned to her. There was a streetlight in front of Mr Thorson's house, directly in front of them, and when she shifted her gaze to look at him, she could see his face quite clearly. He didn't look in the least angry, she saw with some surprise, and the dark eyes were kind.

'All right, Jess,' he said pleasantly. 'I can understand your point of view.' The thin mouth turned up in a brief smile. 'I might even agree with it, in principle.'

'I'm glad to hear that,' she said in a tight voice, just a little annoyed that he'd given up so easily.

'But not in practice,' he went on. 'I'm simply not going to give you up, Jess, and that's flat.'

'But what's the point?' she said. 'I'm not going to have an affair with you, and I won't change my mind.

I simply can't afford it. What else is there for us?'

He spread his hands wide and lifted his broad shoulders. 'Hell, how should I know? Maybe nothing, but I intend to find out.' He took her hand in both of his and turned it over, his eyes fixed on hers in an intent gaze. 'I like you, Jess. I have since that first night, when I came crawling under your window and you took such good care of me.' He raised her hand and placed his lips on the palm. 'My feelings for you go far beyond sex.' The smile quirked again. 'Much as I enjoy that.'

She didn't know what to think, what to say. Was there hope after all? Maybe she wouldn't have to give him up, not entirely. Did she dare allow this man to fill even a corner of her life, feeling the way she did about him?

'What are you suggesting?' she asked weakly.

'Just that we see each other, get to know each other better under more normal conditions.'

'I don't know,' she said, shaking her head slowly. 'I'm afraid.'

His hand tightened around hers. 'Hell, Jess, so am I.'

She gave him a swift glance of disbelief. 'You? Afraid? I didn't think anything in the world frightened you.'

'Only you, Jess,' he said softly. 'Only you.'

She had to laugh. 'I'm no threat to you, Jason. Surely you know that by now.'

He raised one dark eyebrow. 'Oh, no? I've lived my whole adult life pretty much as a loner. Oh, I've had friends and, I'll have to admit, several women not quite as scrupulous as you are about short-term affairs. But I saved the best part of myself for my work. Do you understand?'

'Oh, yes. I understand perfectly. As a matter of fact, if you eliminate the part about the casual affairs, you've pretty much described my own attitude.'

'Right,' he agreed. 'And, like you, this way of life satisfied me. Then along came this wisp of a honey-haired doctor and turned that life upside down. And that scares me.'

Her heart leapt into her throat. In effect, she thought, he's telling me he loves me. Or at least that he could. Can I really let that chance slip by? She made her decision.

'All right,' she said with a sigh. 'Let's try it your way. For a while, anyway, to see what happens.'

'Good,' he said with feeling. Then he added, 'But no bed?'

'No,' came the firm reply. 'No bed.'

He sighed. 'All right. I'd better get you inside, then.'

They got out of the car and walked up the dark path together towards the house. When she had unlocked the front door and switched on the hall light, she turned to say good night to him.

'I'll call you in a day or two,' he said. 'We'll do something sane and sensible and normal.'

He put his arms around her then and kissed her chastely on the mouth. There was no urgency in his embrace, and he didn't prolong it. She was grateful for his restraint. The strong muscles of his arms, even under the woollen jacket, felt too good under her hands, and the pressure of his mouth on hers too tempting, for her to have resisted him if he had pressed her further.

He left her, then, and she stood in the doorway watching him as he walked down the path away from her. When he reached the car, he turned and gave her a little wave before getting in and driving off.

She went inside, shutting and locking the door behind her, and sank back against it happily, the taste of his brief kiss still on her lips.

CHAPTER NINE

IN the weeks that followed, they saw each other at least every other night. Jessica would cook dinner for him occasionally, or they would go out to eat, either driving into Washington or walking the short distance to The Willow Inn. At weekends, they would take long drives through the countryside or just spend the day at her house in front of the fire.

It was early November now, and the spectacular autumn foliage was almost gone, leaving only a few gold or red leaves scattered among the barren branches of the oaks and maples. Soon it would be winter, and the ice and snow would appear.

True to his word, Jason had not pressed her into lovemaking, and although he was attentive and affectionate when they were together, he still limited himself to one good night kiss. In spite of her own good resolutions not to jump into a casual affair with him, she was finding his restraint more than a little frustrating. Although she had learned a lot about him in the past few weeks—his work, the book he was writing about his experiences in San Crístobal, his lonely childhood—she still didn't feel she really knew him. He always kept a part of himself in reserve, a part she couldn't reach, and sometimes she wondered if she would ever really know this man.

It was beginning to dawn on her that the barriers he had so carefully erected around his inner self had only been transcended during their lovemaking, when they were in San Crístobal. He had really come

alive then, but she didn't know whether this was due
to their physical intimacy or the fact that he was only
really in his element when he was hot on the trail of a
story and in a situation of danger.

The fact that they were together almost constantly
didn't escape the notice of the ever-vigilant Lisa, who
confronted her with it one night on the telephone.
Jason was due any minute, and she still had some
last-minute preparations to make for dinner, but she
hadn't spoken to Lisa for several days and didn't like
to cut her short.

After a few minutes of small talk about the weather
and the health of each member of the family, there
was a pregnant pause. Jessica steeled herself, her
instinct and knowledge of her sister-in-law's methods
warning her what was coming.

'I understand you're becoming involved with
Jason Strong,' Lisa said at last.

Jessica laughed. 'Involved? I'm not sure what you
mean by that, Lisa. I've gone out to dinner with him a
few times, that's all.'

This was not quite the whole truth, but she didn't
want Lisa to know the full extent of the relationship.
It was too soon. Neither she nor Jason was sure just
what their their status was or what kind of future they
were heading for. At this point she wasn't entirely
sure they even had a future.

'How long has this been going on?' Lisa persisted.

'Oh, just a few weeks,' Jessica replied airily. 'He's
good company and an interesting man.'

'A dangerous man,' said Lisa drily. 'He's an
adventurer, Jessica. He'll never settle down.'

Jessica's cheeks burned. 'Well, Lisa, can't I go out
with a man without planning to settle down with
him?' She was growing angry, but she was honest

enough with herself to realise that a good part of the reason for her sudden irritation was that Lisa was right. Jason was a dangerous man, an adventurer, and this disturbed her more than she liked to admit.

'Of course you can, darling,' said Lisa in a softer tone. 'I just don't want to see you get hurt.' She paused for a moment. 'What about Marshall Bennett?'

Jessica sighed. She felt guilty enough about Marshall without having Lisa bring it up. He hadn't called since the night of the ball at the French Embassy, more than a month ago. If Lisa knew she was seeing Jason, so would Marshall.

'There was never anything between me and Marshall,' she said weakly.

'Well, Jessica, it's entirely your own affair whom you go out with. You know I don't like to interfere.' Jessica rolled her eyes heavenward at this patent untruth and waited. 'But you're twenty-eight years old,' Lisa went on inexorably. 'It's time you started thinking about marriage, a family. Marshall would make an ideal husband, and I hate to see you wasting your time on a man like Jason Strong, who . . .'

Just then the doorbell chimed. 'Sorry, Lisa,' Jessica broke in. 'Someone's at the door. I'll talk to you later. Goodbye.'

She hung up the phone and ran to the front door. It had been raining all day and was sleeting now as the temperature plunged lower after nightfall. The front porch was covered, but still, as she opened the door, he stood there huddled into his tan trench coat, shivering, the collar turned up, his hair glistening with drops of the icy rain.

As always, the minute he appeared, her heart went out to him, and she literally glowed from head to foot at the mere sight of him. He held out a brown-paper parcel.

'I brought some wine for dinner.'

'Come in. It's awful out there.' When he was inside and she had shut the door, she took the parcel from him. 'Sorry to keep you standing there,' she said, 'but I was on the phone with Lisa giving me some more of her maternal advice.'

He shrugged out of his coat and handed it to her. 'What was she warning you against this time?'

'You,' she replied without thinking.

As she turned to hang up his coat in the hall cupboard, the implications of her off-hand remark were borne in on her. The last thing she wanted was to make him feel she was backing him into a corner. What she longed for, prayed for, was that he would give up his dangerous life so that they could build some kind of future together, but such a decision had to come from him without even a hint of pressure from her.

'I was going to build a fire,' she said brightly when she turned to face him again, 'but then I got stuck on the phone and didn't have time.' She looked at the serious, brooding expression on his face with a little thrill of alarm. 'Maybe you'd like to do that while I finish in the kitchen.'

'All right,' he said and followed her into the living-room.

In the kitchen, as she checked the roast and put the salad she had made earlier into the refrigerator, she cursed herself for her thoughtless comment about Lisa's warning. He hadn't liked it, that much was clear. Maybe it would be all right, she thought, as she took down the wine-glasses from the cupboard. I'll just have to be more careful.

She put the glasses and the bottle of wine he had brought on a tray and carried them into the living-room. He was standing with his back towards her, his arms braced against the mantelpiece, staring down into the flames of the fire he had built.

Once again, her heart went out to him in a yearning, helpless love. He had dressed casually in a pair of black trousers, white turtleneck sweater and a heathery-grey tweed jacket. His dark hair curled over the edge of the sweater at the back of his neck, and she longed to run to him, to plunge her hands into the thick hair, to press herself up against the long, lean body.

Then he turned his head. Their eyes met. Jessica could feel the tray shaking in her hands. He raised a hand and ran it over the back of his neck in an impatient gesture.

'Can the dinner wait a while?' he asked in a low, controlled voice.

'Yes,' she replied. She set the tray down on the coffee-table. 'We can have some wine first.'

Silently, he uncorked the wine, poured it out into the glasses and handed one to her. She took it from him and sat down on the couch. He drank his down quickly, still standing there, then poured himself another.

'I'd like to talk to you,' he said gravely.

Fear clutched at her heart, and she took a sip of wine. He was going to leave her again, she knew it. The newspapers had been full of stories lately about fighting in Nicaragua, another one of those incomprehensible internal battles in war-torn Central America that seemed never to end.

He sat down beside her then, leaning forwards, his arms resting on his thighs, slowly twirling his wineglass around in his long fingers.

'I've been doing a lot of thinking lately, Jess,' he said, without looking at her.

Here it comes, she thought, and braced herself. 'I see,' she said carefully. 'And what was your conclusion?'

'There was no conclusion,' he said. 'Until tonight.' He turned to face her then, his dark eyes hooded, unreadable. 'Then when you let it slip that Lisa was warning you against me, it all fell into place.'

'Jason, I never meant . . .'

'I know that,' he broke in. 'But she was right, and I needed to hear it. It made me understand how unfair I've been to you.'

She took a deep silent breath. 'I'm not complaining,' she said.

'I know you're not, and I appreciate it.' He paused, then looked into the fire. 'The paper wants me to go to Nicaragua,' he said shortly.

There it was, then, what she had feared. She tried to steel herself against the sudden wave of despair that swept over her. It meant the end of everything, all her hopes, all her dreams for the future. The one thing she was certain of was that if he went off again to more danger, it was over between them. She couldn't bear a life of constant dread for his very life whenever he was away from her. It would be better to cut it off now. It was his decision, but he would have to accept her position, too. She tried to make her voice casual.

'When are you leaving?'

He ran a hand distractedly through his hair. 'I'm not,' he said, turning to face her. 'I'm going to turn them down.'

Carefully, she set her glass down on the tray. The

room had begun to whirl as his words sunk in, and her hand was shaking uncontrollably.

'You're going to turn them down?' she repeated in a whisper.

He reached out for her then and gathered her in his arms. She sank against him gratefully and clung to him. His hands moved up and down her back in a frantic, possessive gesture, and he put his mouth at her ear.

'I love you, Jess,' he said in a choked voice. 'I never thought it would happen to me, but I suddenly realised that no story in the world was worth losing you for.'

'Oh, Jason, I love you so much,' she breathed. 'I always have.'

He put his hands on her face and looked down at her. 'Marry me, Jess. I don't know a damn thing about settling down, making a home, having a family, but you can teach me. Say you'll marry me.'

Beside herself with joy, she replied simply, 'Any time. Anywhere.'

He buried his face in her hair, stroking it, and growled into her ear, 'You know what I want, don't you?'

She put her hand inside his jacket and pressed it up against his pounding heart. 'Yes,' she whispered. 'I know. I want it, too.'

He kissed her then, tenderly, lovingly, tasting her, sipping at her lips as though he could never get enough of her. He brushed one hand lightly across her thrusting breasts, then, with a groan, gripped her by the shoulders and levered himself away from her.

'But I'm not going to do it,' he said shakily. 'We're going to do this thing right. Forget what happened in San Cristobal, and march sedately to the altar like two normal people.'

She wanted to cry out to him that she didn't want to forget what happened in San Crístobal, that that's where she fell in love with him, but she stopped herself. He was giving up an important part of his life for her, and she would have to let him do it his way.

'Yes, darling,' she said demurely. 'Whatever you say.'

Jessica floated through the next few weeks on a wave of sheer bliss. Jason was leaving all the wedding decisions to her, and only asked that it be as soon as possible. Lisa was ecstatic at the news and welcomed Jason into the family with open arms, just as though, Jessica thought with wry amusement, she had never issued the warning against him.

Even the phlegmatic Charles seemed delighted and gave his sister a hug and an admiring glance when she told him about it, with the dry comment that he had to hand it to her, he didn't think the woman existed who could tame Jason Strong.

Several times in those blissful weeks, however, when she caught Jason off-guard, she thought she could see a distant, almost haunted look in his eyes. This made her wonder uneasily if he was regretting his decision to give up his exciting life for her. She never mentioned it to him, however, and always, when he became aware that she was watching him, he would smile and reach out for her. She felt safe, then, as he held her in his arms, kissed her and told her how much he loved her. She believed him. There was no mistaking the genuineness of his feelings for her, and the moment would pass.

The only real unpleasantness in those halcyon days was the phone-call she received from Marshall

Bennett one Sunday afternoon just a few days after the announcement of the engagement appeared in the society page of Jason's newspaper.

'I thought I'd call and offer my congratulations, Jessica,' he said stiffly. He gave a dry, humourless laugh. 'Although I think it's considered more proper to offer the bride best wishes and to congratulate the groom.'

'Thank you, Marshall,' she said uncomfortably.

'It was rather sudden, though, wasn't it? You just met a month ago.'

'Well, it was, rather,' she hedged. 'He's a very persuasive man.' There was a dead silence on the line for a few awkward moments. 'Marshall, I'm sorry . . .'

'Oh forget it, Jessica,' he said with a long sigh. 'You never made me any promises or held out any hope.' He laughed again. 'I guess I'm just a sore loser.' He hesitated. 'I only hope you know what you're doing. I've known Jason Strong for some time, now, and like him personally, as well as respecting his ability and courage. But you surely know by now that he's not cut out for domesticity. Do you think you'll be able to tolerate the long absences while he's off on one of his harrowing adventures?'

'He's not going to do that any more,' she said promptly. 'He's giving it all up.'

'I see,' he said. 'I thought . . .' His voice trailed off.

'You thought what, Marshall?'

'Oh, it's nothing, really,' he said uncomfortably. 'I was probably mistaken.'

'Come on, Marshall, it must be something.'

'Well, I was just going to say that I thought he'd be going to Nicaragua shortly. Under the circumstances, that is. But since you say he's given that all up, I guess he's decided not to go.'

'What "circumstances" are you talking about?'

'Jessica, I think you'd better discuss this with Jason. I've already said too much. I'm sure it's nothing, only a rumour. If he told you he wasn't going, you can believe him. I've never known the guy to lie.'

His voice was so firm that Jessica knew it would be pointless to persist. She wouldn't get another word out of him. Besides, it made her feel vaguely disloyal to Jason to discuss him behind his back like this. Marshall had heard a rumour, but he was right. Jason would never lie to her.

'You're right, Marshall,' she said, trying to get a cheerful note into her voice. 'Well, it was nice of you to call, and I really am sorry. You know I'm fond of you, but it just wasn't on the cards.'

'Sure, Jessica. I understand.' Then, just as she was about to say goodbye, he said, 'Oh, by the way, I almost forgot. The director of the overseas medical relief agency called me the other day looking for you. It seems they still haven't found a doctor to replace you down in the village and wondered if you'd consider going back.'

She laughed. 'Not on your life,' she said with feeling.

'That's what I told her. Well, once again, best wishes. I hope you and Jason will be very happy. He's a lucky guy.'

When she had hung up the phone, she stood in the hall with her hand still on the receiver for a long time, still disturbed over the conversation. The first winter snow had fallen last night, and she could hear the muffled sound of tyres crunching on the street outside and the occasional clank of chains as the cars drove slowly by.

Something was going on that Jason hadn't told her about. She remembered those odd moments when she had surprised that haunted look in his eyes, the way he had covered it up. He wouldn't lie to her, she thought fiercely. He wouldn't be planning to go off again after they were married, not when he had promised her he wouldn't.

Whatever it was, he was probably only trying to protect her. Should she let it drop? Or should she confront him? But what with? A vague rumour, that's all. Nothing substantial in the least. If it was anything important, he would tell her about it.

She drove into Washington early that evening to have dinner with him at his apartment as they had planned earlier. The weather had warmed considerably by then, and the last vestiges of snow were gone from the roads. Still, when he opened the door for her, he gave her a worried look.

'You shouldn't have come out in this weather,' he said, ushering her inside and taking her coat. 'I tried to call you, but I guess you'd already left.'

'It's all right now,' she said. 'Besides, a little snow doesn't bother me. I've been driving in it all my life.'

He put his hands on her shoulders and turned her around so that he could kiss her. 'Mm,' he said. 'You taste good. But your hands are freezing. Come in by the fire.'

They walked together into his study, their arms around each other. It was a spartan room, lined with books from floor to ceiling. A huge globe stood in one corner, and a large roll-top desk with a typewriter on top was set against the window wall. At the blazing fire, she turned into his arms and put her hands up against his broad chest.

'You know what they say,' she smiled up at him. ' "Cold hands, warm heart." '

The blue-grey eyes deepened as they gazed down into hers, and he reached out a hand to place it lightly on her breast. She drew in her breath sharply at his touch.

'Just checking,' he said, amused at her reaction. His grasp tightened. 'You do have a warm heart, Jess.'

He lowered his head to kiss her. She put her arms around his waist and pressed up against him, then ran her hands up under his dark sweater to feel the soft warm skin of his back and the hard muscles underneath.

'Are you trying to seduce me?' he murmured against her mouth.

'I—I think so,' she said breathlessly.

He lowered his hands to her hips and pulled her tightly up against him so that she could feel his hard arousal and knew that his desire matched her own.

'If you try hard enough,' he said softly, 'I guarantee you'll succeed.' His open mouth descended on hers then in a deep probing kiss. Then he stepped back and patted her playfully on the behind. 'But not before dinner. I've got a gourmet treat on the stove, and I'm not going to let anything spoil it.'

Flustered, and still highly aroused, she ran a hand shakily through her hair. 'You're a tease, Jason Strong. Do you know that?'

He gave her a long, tender look, still standing a few feet away from her, his own breath laboured. Then he smiled.

'I know I love you, Dr Carpenter.'

She put a hand on his lean bony cheek. 'That's all I need to know.' She dropped her hand. 'Now, let's go see what's cooking in the kitchen.'

His gourmet meal turned out to be a rich tomato stew with beans, highly spiced, *à la* San Crístobal, with a salad of greens and crusty sour-dough bread.

'I hope this doesn't make you homesick for the revolution,' he joked as he dished up the stew.

'It's good, but not that good,' she said, sampling it. 'Oh, that reminds me. Marshall Bennett called this afternoon.'

He gave her a sharp look over the table. 'What did he want?'

'Just to wish me well and to tell me that the agency asked him if I'd consider going back to the village. Seems they haven't found a replacement for me yet.'

'What did you tell him?' he asked carefully.

'Why, I told him no, of course. I informed him that you and I were both going to settle firmly into the domestic life after we're married.' She waited, but he only kept eating in silence. 'We are, aren't we?'

He gave her a quick smile. 'Damned right we are,' he said heartily.

But the heartiness rang false in her ears, and she could tell from his downcast eyes that there was something in them he didn't want her to see. She thought about Marshall's surprise that Jason wasn't going to Nicaragua. There was trouble all over the world. What was so special about Nicaragua?

She realised then that she had to know. Whatever it was, Jason obviously wasn't going to tell her. She would have to prise it out of him. She set her fork down on her plate, put her elbows on the table and leaned forward to catch his eye.

'What's going on in Nicaragua, Jason?' she said quietly.

His hand stilled in mid-air. 'Another revolution, I believe,' he said wryly. 'They never end. You should know that.'

'It's more than that,' she persisted, forcing him to hold her gaze. 'How are you involved? What does it have to do with you?'

She could hear the note of panic rising in her voice and see the sudden look of alarm in his eyes. He shoved his chair back and looked away from her for several seconds. He seemed to be pondering a decision, and she waited, really frightened now, hardly breathing.

'All right,' he said at last with a weary sigh. 'They want me to go to Nicaragua. It seems the leader of the guerrilla forces has finally agreed to give an interview, but he insists on my doing it. In fact, it's a firm condition.'

She stared at him. 'And you're going,' she said flatly.

He banged the palm of his hand down flat on the top of the table so hard that the dishes rattled. Jessica was so startled that her heart jumped into her throat, and she watched, speechless, as he jumped up from his chair and began pacing the room.

'No, damn it,' he ground out at last. 'I'm not going. I turned them down.'

Instantly, a flood of relief washed over her. She opened her mouth to tell him how glad she was, but snapped it shut when she saw him grip the back of his chair and lean over the table, glaring at her with a look that was close to hatred. She shrank back in her chair, her hand at her throat.

'I promised you I'd give all that up,' he snarled,

'and, by God, I'm going to do it.'

His face was twisted as though in an agonising internal struggle. Then, suddenly, it crumpled. He came swiftly to her side and knelt down beside her chair.

'God, I'm sorry, Jess.' He took her hand and raised it to his lips to kiss the palm. 'I'm sorry,' he repeated. 'Forgive me. I didn't mean to take it out on you.' He buried his head in her lap.

Numbly, she reached out a hand and began to stroke the thick dark hair. Her heart was so full of pity and love for him that tears welled up in her eyes. It's costing him too much, she thought sadly. Forcing domesticity on Jason is like putting a magnificent wild panther into a cage. I love him too much to do that to him. It was that very untameable quality in him that had attracted her in the first place.

What should she do? Have an affair with him? Marry him and sit in Taunton waiting for him to come back to her, sick with dread every time she read a newspaper, never knowing if he was dead or alive? Or give him up now, let him go, release him from his promise?

They sat there like that for a long time, his head cradled in her lap while she stroked his head, the back of his neck, in a soothing, gentle rhythm. Finally, she knew what she had to do. Her hands stilled.

'Jason,' she said in a low voice.

He looked up at her, calmer now, the strength she loved back in his face, his eyes, the set of his chin.

'I love you, Jess,' he said.

She smiled. 'I know. And I love you. That's why it can't work between us; surely you see that? It would tear you apart to give up your work. You'd come to hate me for it.' She shook her head sadly. 'I can't do that to you, to us.'

He started to say something, to protest, then instead, he got up and stood with his back to her for several seconds. Everything in her longed to go to him, to feel his mouth on hers again, the long lean body pressed against her, to tell him she wanted him on any terms.

Slowly, she rose to her feet. 'I'm leaving now, Jason.'

He turned, then, his face haggard. 'I *do* love you. You know that. And I'll never forget you.'

With a little sob, she whirled around and ran out of the room.

CHAPTER TEN

JESSICA followed Jason's reports from Nicaragua in the newspaper intently during the next several days. They were absolutely brilliant. What's more, his interviews with the leader of the guerrilla forces seemed to be a powerful factor in resolving the dispute between the two warring factions.

Of course, what he was doing was very dangerous. He was behind the lines, deep in the mountainous guerrilla territory, and there was the constant threat that they might decide to hold him hostage or imprison him, or even kill him if they got the idea he was a spy.

She was so well disciplined that she managed to meet all the demands of her normal life during that trying time. Her construction worker's cast was almost ready to come off, the broken bone in his leg knitting nicely; on the first of December, the young pregnant woman became the mother of a healthy baby boy; and Mrs Columbo's anaemia was showing a slight improvement with the iron shots she was receiving.

Still, Jessica thought late one Friday afternoon as she stood at her office window gazing out at the blanket of snow that had fallen during the day, something vital was missing from her life. What had she really gained, she asked herself, by sending Jason away? How was she better off without him? He was still on her mind constantly, her fears for his safety as agonising to her now as though they'd still planned to marry. Perhaps more so, she added ruefully.

It would be Christmas soon. They were to have been married then. What would have happened if she had released him from his promise yet gone ahead with the wedding? Would that really have been worse than this constant, dull ache in her heart, this absolute void at the centre of her being? At least then she would have had something to look forward to, something tangible.

The last patient of the day was gone. Tomorrow was Saturday. It was Dr Weatherby's turn to be on call. She thought ahead to the blank weekend ahead of her. How could she fill those two empty days that once were filled with Jason's vibrant, exhilarating presence?

That was it, she thought. He was so alive! In spite of his dangerous life, perhaps because of it, he had a certain zest about him that was missing in the other people she knew with their nice safe normal lives, an almost animal pleasure and joy, just by virtue of the fact that he was alive and doing the work he loved, important work, significant work.

I felt like that once, she thought sadly as she stared blindly out at the bleak winter landscape. She hugged her arms in front of her and shivered a little as memories of the village in San Crístobal came flooding back into her mind. Mrs Morales with her fine brood of beautiful, liquid-eyed children, the new baby; little Pablo Silva, hobbling around with his one crude homemade crutch; stoic old Manuel, who never flinched when she had to sew up his hand without an anaesthetic.

She thought of the village square, the children playing in the dust, the women gossiping under the banana trees, the men drinking in the *taverna*, chickens and dogs roaming freely. She thought of the soldiers, brave young boys, most of them, whose lives depended on her medical skills.

Then she heard footsteps coming down the hall towards her office, a heavy tread, and the squeak of rubber-soled shoes on the polished linoleum floor. She turned away from the window to see Mrs Schultz standing at the doorway.

'That's the lot of them, Doctor,' she said briskly. 'I'll be on my way now. Looks like we'll have more snow tonight.'

'Good night, Mrs Schultz,' she said with a smile. 'I'll see you on Monday.'

After she had gone, Jessica collected her things. She had walked to the office that morning. With the snow packed on the streets, it was quicker, and probably safer, than driving. She wandered down the hall, looking into each of the examining rooms, the small lab, the restroom, to make sure everything was in order.

She needn't have bothered, she thought, as she surveyed each spotlessly clean and orderly room. Mrs Schultz was a demon at keeping the office neat and tidy. All the charts were put away in the filing cabinet in the reception area, every instrument in the steriliser and the laundry put in a large canvas bag ready to be picked up on Monday morning.

What a difference from the way she had had to operate in San Cristobal! There she had done it all herself, even to running the laundry through the ancient washing machine downstairs. She had been lucky to have a steriliser at all, and her charts had been kept in a cardboard carton.

I'm getting maudlin, she thought, giving herself a little shake. She marched back to her office to get her

coat and put her boots on. Who would ever have
dreamed, she mused, that I would think with such
affection of that awful place? How could I forget so
soon the fighting, the fear, the constant booming of
the guns?

She sat down to pull on her fur-lined boots. She
knew, of course, that her sudden burst of nostalgia for
the village was entirely due to the fact that that was
where she had met and fallen in love with Jason.
Well, not entirely, perhaps, she amended, but it was
certainly a good part of it, and once again the weak
tears appeared unbidden in her eyes at the thought of
him.

Angrily, she wiped them away and stood up,
pushing her feet more firmly into the boots. I've got
to stop that, she admonished herself sternly with a
loud sniff. All I do lately is cry. Will it never end?

She slipped into her heavy coat and had just gone
to the door when the telephone rang. She hesitated.
All she wanted was to take her misery home and sit in
front of the fire brooding over it. Jason's articles had
stopped abruptly two days earlier, and she was
anxious to see if they had reappeared yet in the
evening paper.

The telephone kept ringing, and finally she
shrugged and decided to answer it. She was still
technically on call until Saturday morning. She
walked over to her desk and picked up the receiver.

'Dr Weatherby's office,' she said.

'May I speak to Dr Carpenter, please? Dr Jessica
Carpenter.' It was a woman's voice, firm and
businesslike.

'This is Dr Carpenter,' she replied, praying it
wasn't an emergency.

'Dr Carpenter, this is Anna Pruett. Perhaps you

remember me?'

Jessica recognised the name instantly as that of the director of the agency which had arranged to send her to San Crístobal, and she was immediately on guard.

'Yes, Mrs Pruett. I do,' she said stiffly.

'I'm sorry to bother you like this,' the woman apologised, 'but I'm desperate. Marshall Bennett told me he'd spoken to you about returning to San Crístobal.'

'Yes, he did,' Jessica answered firmly. 'And I told him that I couldn't possibly consider it. I'm just getting established in a practice here in Taunton. It's out of the question. I'm sorry.'

Mrs Pruett sighed. 'That's what Marshall told me, but I was hoping you might reconsider.' She paused for a moment. 'I can't say I blame you after what you went through down there, but as I say, I'm desperate and decided to give it one more shot.'

'I take it you're still having trouble finding a replacement for me.'

Mrs Pruett laughed drily. 'That's hardly the word. Impossible is more like it.'

'Well, I truly am sorry, Mrs Pruett, but, as I said before, it's out of the question.'

'I understand, Dr Carpenter, and I'm sorry, too. You can't blame me for trying, though.'

'Not at all,' Jessica said politely. 'I hope you find someone soon.'

Ater she hung up, she found that her knees were buckling, her hands trembling, and she sank down into her chair. This is insane, she thought, to get so upset over a phone call! So they need a doctor desperately. Why pick on me? I've already served my time. Why can't they leave me alone?

'This has got to stop,' she said aloud to the empty room. I've got to harden myself against this awful pity, she vowed silently. Between that and losing Jason, I'm going to end up a basket case if I'm not careful.

That evening she scanned the evening paper thoroughly from beginning to end to see if Jason's series of articles had been resumed, but all she found was a short news item that said the cease-fire was still in effect.

She had made a fire as soon as she had arrived home and shed her damp clothes. A light snow had started falling on the way, and walking into the cold empty house was like walking into a tomb. The fire had helped thaw her body out, but her heart was still frozen with apprehension as she searched through the pages of the paper again for some news of Jason. There was nothing.

She stared blankly into the fire, sipping a glass of wine and absently nibbling on the cheese and biscuits she had bought. She hadn't had a decent meal since he had left. Her stomach simply rebelled against anything more substantial than an occasional snack or bowl of soup.

Something has happened to him, she thought bleakly. I know it. Her anxiety threatened to rise out of control as she conjured up visions in her mind of Jason lying wounded and bloody on some distant, alien mountainside, all alone, without even the thought of her love to comfort him.

'Oh, God, what have I done?' she wailed aloud. She covered her face with her hands, in a real panic now, and sobbed brokenly.

Finally, when she had herself under control, she

decided she had to do something. She couldn't just sit
there, helpless, caught in a web of horrible fantasy,
not knowing. But what? What can I do?

I'll call Marshall, she decided. He knows everything that's going on all over the world with his
connections. He had known about Jason's assignment from the beginning. With renewed hope, she
ran into the hall, fumbled in the book for his number,
then dialled it with trembling fingers.

He finally answered on the seventh ring.

'Marshall, it's Jessica,' she said breathlessly.

'Jessica? Is something wrong? I was just on my
way out and almost didn't answer the phone. How
are . . .?'

'Marshall,' she broke in. 'What do you know about
Jason? There haven't been any more of his articles in
the newspaper. Has something happened to him?'

She waited, hardly daring to breathe, but he was
silent for so long that she began to think the
connection had been broken.

'Marshall? Are you still there?'

'Yes,' he replied at last. 'I'm still here. Listen,
Jessica, there's really nothing I can tell you.'

'You mean because you don't know anything, or
because you won't?'

'It's not that simple,' he hedged uncomfortably.
'I've heard some rumours, but nothing definite,
nothing official.'

'Well, tell me the rumours, then!' she cried. Once
again, panic threatened. I must be calm, she told
herself. 'Please, Marshall. I've got to know.'

He sighed wearily. 'All I really know is that for
some reason, he's incommunicado. It could be
anything. You know what it's like down there.
Communications are haphazard at best. Outside of a

few cities, it's a pretty primitive place.'

'All right,' she said calmly. 'Now tell me the rumours.'

'Good Lord, Jessica, take your pick. I've heard everything from stories about his having joined the guerrilla forces to . . .' His voice trailed off.

To his death, she added silently. 'Will you tell me what your honest opinion is, then, Marshall? Off the record.'

Again he hesitated a long time before replying. 'Okay, Jessica, I'll give it to you straight. The most persistent rumour, and the one I'm inclined to believe, knowing the risks he takes and the volatile situation down there, is that they've probably killed him. I could be wrong, you understand,' he added hastily. 'There has been no official word. But if they were going to hold him hostage, we surely would have received their terms by now. If he was only wounded, or ill, they would have got him out for medical attention.'

'I see,' she said in a tight, controlled voice. 'Thank you, Marshall. If you do hear anything definite, will you please let me know?'

'Of course I will. I'm really sorry, Jessica, but you'll have to admit that he knew what he was getting into. Are you sure you'll be all right?'

'Yes. I'm fine.'

They hung up then, and Jessica walked unseeing, unthinking, unfeeling, back to the fire. She just sat there on the couch, staring blankly into the flames, until they faded into a mass of charred embers, then died entirely.

Hardly moving, she dozed fitfully on and off all that night on the couch. By morning's first pale light she was stiff and cramped. She felt exhausted, even more tired than she had been the night before, drained of energy, of will, of hope.

He's dead, she said to herself, as she slowly rose to her feet and stretched painfully. She walked over to the window and gazed out at the snow-covered street. There was no sign of life. Not a car, not a living soul, not even a bird in the barren trees. I know he's dead, she repeated soundlessly.

She could still find no news of him on Monday or Tuesday, even though she scanned the newspaper more thoroughly than she ever had in her life. On both days, she made her early morning hospital rounds and saw her patients in the office as usual. The necessary concentration helped get her mind off him during the day, but she still had the empty evenings to fill and slept fitfully.

The snow had miraculously melted, leaving a sodden, dingy mess behind, and it had rained steadily since Sunday, a depressing constant drizzle that lowered her flagging spirits to the point where she could hardly bear it.

She was becoming so distraught, she realised at last, that she was afraid she might start making mistakes with her patients. She couldn't risk that for a moment. Finally, on Tuesday night, she called Marshall again, just to be doing something.

'There's still no official word,' he replied cautiously to her request for information. 'But the rumours are still flying.'

'What rumours?'

'Well, there's some talk in diplomatic circles about the possibility of government intervention.'

'What does that mean?' she asked in a tight voice.

'Very little, actually, except that we would insist on

some concrete evidence that he's still alive.'

'Wouldn't that rouse some response?' she asked hopefully.

'It's hard to tell, and you shouldn't get your hopes up. It's really just a token gesture, with no real muscle behind it. We're not going to go to war with Nicaragua over one American journalist.'

'I see.' Something in Marshall's tone of voice alarmed her. He was speaking of Jason as though he were already dead. 'You don't think he's still alive, do you, Marshall?' she asked dully.

'Jessica, I just don't know. I do think, however, that you should be prepared for the worst. I'm sorry to have to tell you this, but you've been pretty adamant about wanting to know. And remember, there's no solid evidence one way or the other. It just looks bad, that's all.'

After she had thanked him and hung up, she stood in the hall for several moments staring down at the telephone and digesting the depressing and inconclusive information he had given her. When she raised her eyes briefly, she caught a glimpse of her reflection in the mirror hanging on the wall opposite her.

I look like a wreck, she thought with a jolt of disgust. She had hardly glanced in a mirror for the past three days, and was shocked at the pathetic, woebegone expression on her face, the dejected slump of her shoulders, the dark circles under her eyes.

She gave the unpleasant image a hard look. Is this the girl, she asked herself, who fought her way through medical school and kept her head in a revolution? More to the point, she added, is this the girl Jason Strong had fallen in love with?

'No, damn it!' she cried aloud. She stamped her

foot and her heartbeat picked up its tempo as an idea began to form in her mind. She started pacing through the house from one room to another, excitement building inside her with every step.

She found herself in the kitchen and absently reached up into the cupboard for a can of soup. As she opened it and set it on the stove to warm, she mentally considered where her line of reasoning was leading her.

What good is it doing me to sit here in Taunton waiting for word, wringing my hands like some Victorian maiden whose lover has gone off to battle? Is that really the kind of person I am? There must be something I can do.

When the soup was heated, she stood at the kitchen stove eating it out of the pan, her thoughts still racing madly, until finally, by the time she was through, her idea had become a firm resolve.

She set the pan in the sink and ran water into it, then marched back to the telephone in the hall. As she dialled Marshall's number, she gazed once again at her reflection in the mirror. Already her eyes looked brighter, her shoulders straighter, and the pathetic expression was gone.

'Marshall, I'm sorry to bother you again,' she said after he had answered. 'Do you know how to get hold of Mrs Pruett from the medical agency?'

'You mean tonight?'

'Yes.'

'Uh, I think so. Let's see.'

She waited silently while he looked for the number. She felt oddly detached from herself, as though observing her thoughts and actions from a distance.

'Okay, I've got it,' came Marshall's voice. After he gave her the number, he paused for a moment, then said, 'Do I dare ask why you want to talk to Mrs Pruett?'

'Why, I'm going to tell her I've decided to go back to San Cristobal after all,' she said calmly.

'You what!' he roared. 'Jessica, are you out of your mind?'

'Possibly,' she replied cheerfully. 'I only know I've got to do it. I can't just sit around here moping and waiting any longer. Besides, I want to go.'

For the first time since she had actually decided on her rash course, she realised that this was true. Jason's trouble had given her the impetus she needed, the momentum to take the necessary action, but the desire to go back to a place where she was so desperately needed had been building for months. She just hadn't seen it.

'I don't believe you,' said Marshall. 'What about your practice?'

She laughed. 'Marshall, there are literally hordes of young doctors just waiting in line for an opportunity to step into a practice like Dr Weatherby's. It's an intern's dream. He could find a good replacement for me tomorrow.'

'And you're going to give it all up to go chasing off to Central America looking for Jason Strong? That's crazy, Jessica. You can't possibly hope to find him.'

'Oh, of course not, Marshall,' she said impatiently. 'Don't be silly. I have no intention of trying to find him, but I will be that much closer. I'd appreciate it very much if you'll let him know I'm down there as soon as you get word where he is.'

'Jessica,' he said softly. 'What if he's dead?'

She shut her eyes tight and took a deep breath. 'If he's dead,' she said slowly, 'my life will be over anyway. I might as well spend what's left of it where I can do some good.'

Two weeks later, she was back in San Crístobal. A polite young attaché from the embassy met her at the airport and drove her up the dusty mountainous roads to the village in what looked like the same jeep Marshall used to drive.

There had been a long lull in the fighting, he informed her on the way, and they were hopeful the dispute had been settled at last, but you never knew, he added. There was always the possibility that the fighting would break out again any day.

The word had spread quickly among the villagers that she was coming back, and when the jeep pulled up in front of the house, several of them clustered around it laughing and shouting out their welcomes to her. Her heart warmed towards them, and the display of genuine affection only confirmed her decision.

'You were here once before, weren't you?' the young attaché asked as he helped carry her luggage into the house. 'They seem awfully glad to see you back.' He shook his head. 'You're a brave lady. You must like it here.'

'Yes,' she said with a smile. 'I guess I do.'

When he was gone, she unpacked her belongings and went down to start putting the surgery in some kind of order. As she worked, it seemed to her as though she had never left, that the months she had spent in Virginia were the dream and this the reality. Even now, some of the children were standing outside with their noses pressed up against the surgery window staring in at her.

She had had only one moment of doubt, three days before she left, when, suddenly, Jason's articles had reappeared in the newpaper, and she knew he was still alive. Not only that, but his interviews with the guerrilla leader had been instrumental in creating a real breakthrough in negotiations for a permanent truce with the government. She wondered then if she hadn't done a foolish thing to give up her practice and go back into almost certain danger. Jason was safe. Was there any more reason for her to go?

Yes, she had decided at last. A compelling reason. Quite simply, she was needed. Taunton would always be provided with good medical service. In San Crístobal she was all they had. She knew, too, that it was even more than that. The safe life she had wanted so badly had begun to pall even before the break with Jason. Perhaps, after all, she craved life in the fast lane as much as he did.

Later that evening, she stood on the front step of the house looking out at the familiar square and listening to the monkeys high up in the banana trees as they started their nightly chatter. It would soon be dusk. She felt very peaceful, and had to smile to herself as she recalled her final conversation with Charles and Lisa when they had driven her to the airport just that morning.

'But, darling,' Lisa had wailed, 'Jason is perfectly all right. There's no need for you to go now.'

To Jessica's intense surprise, Lisa had taken the news that she was going back to San Crístobal with astounding grace. A true romantic, it seemed to thrill her to the bones to think of Jessica running off to be close to the man she loved while he was in peril of his life.

Once it became known, however, that he was not only alive and well, but was doing his job effectively, she saw no reason for her to leave.

'I *want* to go back,' she had explained patiently as they stood around waiting for the plane to arrive. 'It's where I belong.' She had given her brother a pleading look. 'Charles, do you understand?'

He had puffed on his pipe and shaken his head. 'Not really, Jessie. I do know, though, that we all have to follow the dictates of our own hearts.' He had patted her fondly on the shoulder and given her cheek a light peck. 'So long as you do that, you'll be all right.'

There was work to be done here, she thought fiercely as the last rays of the setting sun sank behind the tall mountains. It's where I belong, where I want to be. If Jason still wants me, he'll know where to find me.

That night, just before she went to bed, she stood at the door to the bedroom where he had slept while he was recovering from his wound. As she looked inside at the bare room, the neatly made bed, just as he had left it, a host of memories came flooding back into her mind. Jason lying there wounded and feverish in his filthy, blood-stained clothes; the night she had awakened him from the nightmare and stayed with him for the first time; all the succeeding nights on that same bed wrapped in his arms.

Would he come back to her? Would he understand when he found out where she was that she had made a fundamental change in her views, that the conflict between them had been resolved, at least in her mind? All she could do was wait.

CHAPTER ELEVEN

WHEN he did finally come, it was when she least expected it. It was a week after she had arrived back in the village, and she was in the surgery early in the morning before her first patient was due, setting out her instruments and looking over her charts, when he simply appeared in the doorway.

At the sound of the front door quietly opening and closing, she glanced up from the chart she was reading, and there he was, tall, deeply tanned and splendid. Their eyes met and held together for several moments, as great waves of relief and joy flooded through her.

'I was in the neighbourhood,' he said, 'and I thought I'd stop by.'

She put one hand over her heart, as though to still its violent pounding, and sat there, stunned, staring at him, unable to utter a word. He looked wonderful, she thought, in his rumpled khaki and heavy jungle boots. His hair was too long, as usual, and fell in a dark wave over his forehead.

He seemed self-composed, a half-smile quirking the thin mouth, his head slightly tilted to one side looking at her with a faint air of amusement. But the eyes, a deep smoky blue, told her that he, too, was moved by the meeting.

He seemed to be waiting for something. He stood quite motionless, one hand propped against the doorway, the other shoved in his trousers pocket. Then she remembered. She had been the one to send him away. He was waiting for her.

Blindly, she stumbled to her feet, heedless of the charts spilling on to the tiled floor.

'Jason,' she breathed. 'I knew you were alive.' She took a step towards him, but stopped when she saw the sudden frown darken his lean face.

'Is that why you came back?' he said quietly.

She knew immediately what he was asking her. Had she rushed down to San Crístobal out of a feeling of guilt, of concern for his safety, or had it been a rational decision based on her own personal needs? The tension flowed out of her, and she smiled.

'Not entirely,' she said, walking toward him. 'Your articles had begun to reappear in the newspaper before I left Virginia, so I was fairly certain you were all right. But I've been here a week with no news at all, and I knew you were still in danger.'

She was standing before him now, so close that she could see the fine lines around his eyes, the faint stubble on his chin, and the pulse that beat at the hollow of his throat.

'I think we'd better have a talk,' he said.

He ran a hand over his hair in a weary gesture. He looked hot and dirty and worn out. He was probably also hungry.

She glanced at her watch. 'My first patient isn't due for a couple of hours. Why don't you shower and shave, and I'll make you some breakfast.'

He nodded briefly. 'Sounds like a good idea.'

As they walked up the stairs together, she thought about the first night he had come here, wounded and bleeding, and she had had to help him climb these same stairs.

'How did you get here?' she asked when they reached the upstairs landing.

'By plane from Managua, then I borrowed a jeep from the Embassy.'

She noticed that as usual he carried no luggage, only what he had on his back, and she wanted to ask him if he planned to stay. But now was not the time.

She turned to face him. 'You know where everything is,' she said with a smile.

While she cooked his breakfast, she could hear him moving around in his old bedroom, then the sound of the shower running, and she was filled with a vibrant happiness. She didn't know whether he would go or stay or even how he felt about her. For now, though, he was here, and that was all that mattered.

He appeared in the doorway just as she was setting his plate on the table. He had shaved, and his hair was still damp. He was dressed in a pair of the shabby jeans from the box in the cupboard, his broad, tanned chest bare. Her throat closed up at the sight of him.

'Perfect timing,' she said.

As he crossed to the table and sat down, she could smell his clean soapy scent and see the drops of water he had missed still clinging to his shoulders. She drew in her breath sharply, then poured herself a cup of coffee and sat opposite him, hardly able to take her eyes from him. He ate silently for a while, then set his fork down and raised his eyes to her.

'Why have you come back, Jess?'

She thought for a minute, choosing her words carefully. 'I came back because I wanted to,' she said at last.

'That's no answer. Why did you want to?'

She was suddenly shy under his penetrating gaze. He seemed so cold to her, and she began to wonder if she had been mistaken to think he would understand. Still, she had to try.

'At first,' she said, 'it was probably sheer instinct. I didn't know if you were alive or dead, and I guess I had the wild idea that if I were down here, closer to you, somehow I might be able to do something. Oh, I know it was crazy,' she rushed on when she saw the incredulous look on his face. 'Don't laugh. I wasn't thinking straight at the time.'

'I'm not laughing at you,' he said. 'Go on.'

She put her elbows on the table and took a sip of coffee. 'Then, gradually, it began to seem the right thing to do all by itself, simply on its own merits.'

'What about your nice safe life?' he asked, his voice rising. 'What about your longing to settle down? That's why you sent me away, refused to marry me. Remember?'

He seemed almost angry, and she began to shrivel inside as a little knot of fear formed at the pit of her stomach. He had a right to be bitter, she thought sadly. Maybe it was too late. But he had come to her, she thought fiercely, and plunged on.

'Yes,' she said, 'I remember. I told you I wouldn't be able to tolerate a life of constant worry over your safety. I thought it would be better, easier, safer for me if you were out of my life entirely.' She set her cup down and gazed into his eyes. 'I was wrong.'

A gleam appeared in the dark-blue depths. 'Are you sure?' he said in a low voice.

She nodded her head vigorously. 'Absolutely. My life is nothing without you, Jason,' she said, her last vestige of pride gone.

Her voice cracked then on a strangled sob. She stumbled to her feet and ran to him, kneeling beside his chair, and buried her head in his lap. He stroked her hair and murmured her name, soothing her, gentling her, until finally she raised her head and gazed up at him.

'Jason, I thought you were dead,' she wailed.

He put his large warm hands on her face and wiped the tears with his thumbs. 'What would you have done, then, Jess? Gone back to your safe life?'

She shook her head. 'No. Without you I have no life, no safety. I had decided before I left that I'd go through with my plans no matter what happened to you.'

He smiled then. 'What about all those tomorrows you were so worried about?' he asked softly.

'There may not even be a tomorrow,' she replied firmly. 'Today is what counts, and today you're here, with me.'

The hands on her face stilled as he gazed down at her. Then the fingers of one hand brushed lightly over her mouth. He rose slowly to his feet, bringing her with him, and they stood facing each other.

'I love you, Jess,' he said in a deep voice. 'I still want to marry you, but I can't give up my life, my work.'

'No, darling,' she said, her heart singing. 'And neither can I. My work is here. Yours is wherever it takes you. I love you not in spite of who you are, but because of it.'

His arms came around her then and he pulled her closely to him. He pressed his face against hers and began to murmur in her ear.

'I want you so badly, Jess. Say you want me, too.'

'Oh, I do, Jason. It's all I want.'

She felt as though she was floating mindlessly, able only to give herself up to the present moment, and she sank against him. His hand was moving up and down her bare arm in a soothing, hypnotic rhythm, and she laid her head on his shoulder with a sigh.

He slowly lowered his head. She closed her eyes, waiting, and when his lips touched hers, a deep joy filled her. His mouth was soft, brushing lightly over hers in a slow, sensuous motion at first. Then, suddenly, as though they both burst into flame at once, they clutched blindly at each other and clung together in a frantic embrace.

Wordlessly, still locked together, they moved slowly out of the kitchen and down the hall to Jason's old bedroom. When they reached the side of the bed, she turned into his arms and raised her face. Their lips met again, and as they sank down on the edge of the bed, his mouth opened over hers in a sudden urgency.

Under the force of his kiss, she lowered her head back on the pillows. He leaned over her, his hot tongue probing and insistent, demanding entrance. With no thought except for him, she surrendered to him totally. As his tongue explored her mouth, his hands moved over her body possessively, from her shoulders over her breasts, then down to her thighs and back up under her skirt. It was as though he wanted to memorise every inch of her.

He tore his mouth away then and pressed his cheek against hers, so that she could feel his hot rasping breath in her ear. He was lying half on top of her now, their thudding hearts beating in unison.

'God, what you do to me, Jess!' he breathed harshly. He raised his head, his dark eyes boring into her. 'There hasn't been a day that I haven't wanted you.'

With their eyes still locked together, he brushed one hand lightly over her breasts, then slipped it underneath her thin blouse to rest on her bare midriff. His touch on her skin sent a shaft of liquid fire coursing through her bloodstream. She moaned faintly and closed her eyes as his hand moved slowly upwards, then she sighed deeply when it closed around her breast.

'Sit up,' he whispered, guiding her to an upright position so that she sat facing him.

He tugged upwards on the loose blouse, and she raised her arms so that he could slip it over her head. When she was free of it and he had dropped it behind him at the foot of the bed, he held her arms in place with one hand, while with the other he trailed his long fingers down her upraised arm and bent his head to lay his lips on her bare shoulder.

'Touch me,' he said, pulling back from her and releasing her arms.

Eagerly, she reached out both hands to run them lightly, tantalisingly, over the lithe sinewy muscles of his strong arms and broad chest. As her fingers trailed lower, fluttering on his flat abdomen, he sucked in a deep breath, and she could feel the muscles quivering under her touch. He reached behind her then to unclasp her bra and slip it off.

'You're as beautiful as I remember you,' he said with wonder in his voice.

He placed his large hand over one bare breast, then the other, moving back and forth slowly, first kneading, then barely touching, until she threw her head back groaning at the sheer pleasure of it.

He bent his head then and opened his lips over one taut, thrusting nipple, drawing on it, pulling it inside the warm moist interior of his mouth, his tongue flicking over it, while his hands slid lower, beneath the waistband of her skirt.

She was filled with a wild elation, a mindless ecstasy, and could barely suppress a glad cry of joy.

She clutched at the dark head at her breast, her
fingers raking through the crisp dark hair. His greedy
mouth shifted to her other breast, his hands slipped
down lower, and she arched her body upwards to feel
the full force of his own arousal.

With a low groan deep in his throat, he left her
again to pull off the worn jeans. Before he came back
to her, he undid the fastening of her skirt and slid it
down over her hips, his fingers lingering along the
way on her stomach, her thighs, her legs. He covered
her body with his, his breath coming in great racking
gasps now. She put her arms around his neck and ran
her fingers through his thick hair.

He raised his head, hovering over her for a
moment, staring down at her, clasping her face in his
hands.

'I love you, Jess,' he ground out.

With a low moan, she pulled his head down to kiss
him, and then, once again, they became one, joined
together in the deepest expression of love.

Some time later, Jessica lay beside the man she loved
watching him sleep. He was exhausted from his long
journey. She would have to get up soon, get dressed
and go down to the surgery to wait for her first
patient. It was beginning to look as though there
might be another little Morales on the way.

Listening to his deep steady breathing, she gazed
her fill at the long, lithe body lying next to her, half-
covered by the tangled sheet. His dark head was
turned slightly away from her on the pillow so that his
strong features were in profile, the long thick lashes
resting on the high cheekbones, the persistent lock of
hair falling almost to his eyes.

A great surge of love for him rose up in her, so

powerful that she could barely contain it. She didn't know how long he would stay or where he would go when he left or what kind of future they would have together. All she knew was that it had to be with him.

They would marry, of course, she thought dreamily, just as they had once planned. That was understood. Maybe even have children. She would like that, and she imagined tall sturdy replicas of the man lying beside her. She knew there were times when his work would take him from her and he would be in danger, but a love like theirs would have to be a lifetime commitment, whatever the price.

He was here with her today, and whether they were together or apart, all her tomorrows would be his.

ROMANCE

Loving

Little Heather Fraser had everything she could possibly want, except the love of her father, Jay.

His callousness shocked the tiny Cotswold village, and most of all Claire Richards, whose daughter Lucy was Heather's friend.

When Jay accused Claire of encouraging the girls' friendship so that she could see more of *him*, nothing could have been further from the truth.

A freak accident suddenly put paid to Claire's cherished independence. Would she be able to swallow her angry pride and reluctantly share the Frasers' roof?

After 25 million sales worldwide, best-selling author Penny Jordan presents her 50th Mills & Boon romance for you to enjoy.

Available January 1987
Price £1.50.

Mills & Boon